Napoleon Xylophone

Frank Lambert

Matador
9 Priory Business Park
Kibworth Beauchamp
Leicestershire LE8 0RX, UK
Tel: (+44) 116 279 2299
Fax: (+44) 116 279 2277
Email: books@troubador.co.uk
Web: www.troubador.co.uk/matador

ISBN 978 1780882 628

British Library Cataloguing in Publication Data.
A catalogue record for this book is available from the British Library.

Typeset in Minion Pro by Troubador Publishing Ltd

Matador is an imprint of Troubador Publishing Ltd

For Michael,
and any other Whizz Kid looking for a different kind of hero.

N
a
p
Xylophone
l
e
o
n

You are thinking in human terms again and forgetting Time is neither tick nor tock...
Jarle Heavyfoot

Mandrake Ackx stopped listening to Time falling restless and focused his attention on the biometric lock. How human technology had advanced, how easy it remained to overcome. He placed his skeletal finger on the panel and his fingerprint began to alter until it matched precisely the one stored inside the lock's feeble memory.

As the door swung inwards, Ackx entered the narrow passageway with the changeling padding along beside him. Stepping into the elevator at the end of the hallway he looked down at the panel and pressed the button marked X, knowing it would take him where he needed to be, despite the fact he had never been in the building before. As the elevator slowly began to creak into life, Ackx closed his eyes and waited. His eyes itched. They always itched whenever he left the underworld. It wasn't just the sun; the air in Newcastle City Centre was dry too, even when it rained. He wanted to sleep, to keep his eyes closed and feel the itching disappear. He couldn't sleep just yet though, not until he had put things in place.

The creaking continued even when the elevator stopped and Ackx opened his eyes, then pulled the doors open, seeing that he had been taken to an apartment. There was nothing of interest inside. No human life or signs of underworld innovation. The tall windows left and right allowed light to stream into the space; Ackx instinctively pulled up the lapels of his jacket to cover his neck and placed his hands inside his pockets.

'Find him,' Ackx's shrill voice ordered the four-legged beast by his side.

The changeling closed its perfectly white eyes and opened its perfectly grotesque jaws. A long, reptilian tongue flicked out of its mouth and licked the air. When it opened its eyes once more it darted towards a door at the far end of the apartment, on legs that looked too short to carry its powerful body. Stopping at the door, it began to whimper like it was about to be beaten by a cruel master.

Ackx strode bare-footed towards the door but before he reached it, the door silently opened inwards. Without breaking stride, Ackx walked through the doorway and into the workshop at the other side. He was pleased to see there were no windows; all of the light inside was artificial. Leaning against the walking cane, crafted from his father's shinbone an age ago, he stared at his old friend and wondered why he had let so much time slip by without hunting him down sooner.

Eli didn't look up when Ackx entered. Instead, he continued to check the circuit board clamped in the crocodile clips with the test meter he held. He was a short man who appeared even shorter than his true height, hunched like he was over the circuit board. He looked tired and older than the seventy-three birthdays he had sometimes celebrated, sometimes forgot. His long, grey hair hung lank and his beard looked like it had been growing from the moment he had been born.

'Why are you here, Mandrake?' he sighed, staring through the loupe attached to his head with a delicate brass strap.

'I'm here for something we both want,' Ackx replied. 'I want you to come back and work for me.'

Eli shook his head and put the test meter on the workbench. 'You know I will never work for you again,' he said, unclamping the circuit board while carefully holding it by its edges.

'I know you will never willingly work for me again.'

Eli turned around, pulling the loupe away from his eye, but still not looking at Ackx. He walked across to a platform where a wheelchair that looked like it had been created by designers from the future stood almost complete.

'So why are you here?'

Ackx removed the horn-rimmed sunglasses he had been wearing and placed them in the chest pocket of his severely creased jacket. 'I see you are still working on the wheelchair for your grandson. How old is he now?'

'What do you want, Mandrake?'

A grin that might have been a grimace crossed Ackx's face and disappeared almost as soon as it appeared. 'I need you,' he said, unconvincingly.

'A wyte needing a human.' Eli pressed his finger on the armrest's biometric pad and a panel slid across, revealing a small keyboard underneath. 'That must be a first.' He tapped a number sequence in the keypad and ended the sequence with the letter X. The armrest slid forward with a low motorised hum and Eli placed the circuit board in the connector below, before pushing the armrest back into place.

'You would not have all of this if it was not for me,' Ackx said, sweeping his arms around, indicating the workshop and much more.

'I could sleep at night if it was not for you,' Eli said, turning towards Ackx for the first time and immediately wishing he hadn't the moment he did. Ackx's black eyes were too beautiful, too cruel.

'I still need to speak to Time,' Ackx smiled.

'You're a fool if you think I'll work on that project again.' Eli turned away from Ackx, facing the wheelchair and checking it over one final time.

'What about your grandson?'

'What about him?'

'Does he have your ingenuity?'

'No.'

'Maybe he needs a helping hand to awaken his potential.'

Eli turned back towards Ackx and this time he did not flinch. 'Leave Napoleon out of this.'

Ackx pulled back his lips, revealing needle-like teeth that had yellowed with age. He angled his head and began to pick at the gaps in his teeth with his fingernail. 'But I need someone to work for me.'

Facing the wheelchair once more, Eli typed – *Napoleon Mode* – into the keyboard before sliding the cover shut. He stepped down from the platform and faced Ackx. 'I can't leave Napoleon on his own.'

'Then bring him along.'

Eli shook his head from side to side. 'I'll leave him a message,' he said, pulling a mobile phone, that looked more like a brick, from his lab coat pocket.

'You are going to work for me without putting up a fight?'

Eli began to slowly type a message in the phone's oversized keys, then suddenly stopped. 'Where is Hestia?' he asked.

Ackx bared his teeth in response.

Deleting the message he had written, Eli started to type a new one. Before he had finished typing his message, Ackx was at his side. 'It's not that I don't trust you. It's just that I don't trust myself.' Ackx said, taking the phone from Eli just as he pressed send. Ackx dropped the phone on the floor and it bounced twice before coming to a halt at the base of the platform.

Moving away from Ackx, Eli reached inside his pockets and pulled out a pair of shining, metallic gloves. He put the gloves on and then twisted an electrical isolator switch on the panel he now stood next to.

Ackx watched him unconcerned but the changeling followed Eli with unblinking eyes and began to snarl, guttural and malevolent. When the wheelchair bleeped twice, the changeling shapeshifted into half leopard, half hyena and sprang towards the old man in response. As the beast's front paws landed on Eli's shoulders, its hind legs curled up, ready to rip out his stomach with its now fully extended claws.

Eli fell back against the panel, knocking his head as he did. At the same time he grabbed hold of the beast with his gloved hands and needle-like spikes suddenly extended from them. As the spikes dug into the beast's flesh, a charge of electricity surged from the spikes into the changeling and it recoiled away from Eli, crashing against the panel and screeching as it writhed on the floor. Tiny electrical threads sparked over its body, like phosphorescent worms squirming in sequence, and yellow slime oozed from the changeling where the spikes had pierced its skin. A foul stench began to fill the air and Eli watched as the changeling began to morph into a hairless, gorilla-like creature with a featureless expression. It suddenly stopped whining and gingerly picked itself up before limping over to Ackx's side with its head bowed. It licked the skin where it bled and fine metallic fur started to cover it until it shimmered, like a night time lake reflecting the light from a full moon.

Standing up unsteadily, Eli placed his hand on the side of his head and when he removed it he saw there was blood on the, now spike-less, glove.

'There you go again, Eli, reinforcing my belief in you with your clever gadgets,' Ackx laughed and it felt like a bitter wind sweeping through the workshop. He walked towards Eli all wrong, with faltering, disjointed movements, exactly the way a wyte moves when it is over excited.

Despite not wanting to appear weak, Eli shrank away from Ackx.

'Don't worry old friend,' Ackx said, as he placed a hand on Eli's shoulder. 'I am not here to hurt you. I am here to take you home.'

As Ackx ushered Eli out of the apartment, a Tarsier monkey sitting inside a goldfish bowl, left precariously balanced on top of a pile of books on the floor, watched them leave the apartment. Its huge, unblinking eyes glinted curiosity and its head turned like an owl as it followed the path they took. When they were gone, it closed its eyes and waited for the boy, like it had been instructed to do many years before.

2

Zam checked the message on his phone for the second time, puzzled by what he read. Then he checked who sent it again. 'I've got a text from Grandfather,' he said, 'I've never had a text from him before. Even when he sends a text, he still calls me Napoleon. How many times do I have to tell him I hate that name?'

'What does he want?' Ezzy asked.

'He told me not to come home.'

'You mean not to come home in the next half hour or so?'

'I don't know. All it says is "Napoleon, don't come home".'

'That's an odd thing to say?'

'Grandfather is always odd.'

'Yes, I like that about your grandfather,' Ezzy laughed.

A blue polecat stuck its head out of Zam's jacket pocket and sniffed the air. Unimpressed with the bland scents of the railway station, it quickly ducked back into the pocket and went to sleep. Zam had named the polecat Rat, after mistaking it for a rat the day his grandfather first brought it home. *"I found it on a swing in the park,"* Grandfather had said by way of an explanation.

Rat hadn't always been blue; his fur only changed to that colour when his curious nature found him sniffing around a bucket of liquid Grandfather was experimenting with. The liquid was meant to be a mood dye – depending upon a person's mood, their hair would change colour to suit their frame of mind. Grandfather said he never knew what mood Zam was in and he was going to do something about it so he didn't have to keep asking him. Grandfather's experiment hadn't quite turned out the way he expected, though, and Rat's fur remained blue ever since that day, despite his mood. Not all of his fur turned blue; a band around his snout stayed white as well as the two slashes above his black eyes that were shaped like arched eyebrows and made him appear as if he was continually questioning things. His claws, too, were white.

And Zam, once he realised the colour stayed forever, dyed his hair blue because it meant no one could change it. At least, not until Grandfather saw what he had done and then made some dye as black as black could be – Zam's normal hair colour. Later, after he'd worked on Grandfather, he had more choice. Now, his long hair was black and red, because no one else at school had their hair that way and sometimes people stared at him because of his hair, not his wheelchair.

He wondered what Ezzy would look like with red hair?

Distracted when the Cranberries started to sing *Zombie* on her phone, Ezzy didn't notice the crack in the walkway and when the small front wheel of Zam's wheelchair hit the crack, it twisted and brought them to an abrupt halt.

'Sorry,' Ezzy said.

They were in Durham for the Steampunk Festival. Zam wanted to get his grandfather something special for his birthday in a few weeks' time. He found the perfect gift when they came across a furniture stall and the owner showed him a curvaceous rocking chair made from darkened walnut that had a velvet seat a peculiar shade of purple. Grandfather loved peculiar things and Zam bought the chair, asking for it to be delivered on the morning of his grandfather's birthday.

Everything had been fine until they left the festival and two youths drinking beer outside a pub stared at Zam. When they started to laugh and make comments about the way Ezzy was too good-looking to be wheeling a freak like Zam around, the afternoon turned miserable and Ezzy knew it was time for them to return to Newcastle.

'You need to look where you're going,' Zam complained.

Ezzy checked the message on her mobile with one hand as she tried to pull the wheelchair out of the crack with the other.

'I was looking, I just didn't see.'

'You need new eyes then.'

'And you need a new tongue, so you can speak nicely for a change.'

'Just hurry up and get us to the train. I want to know what Grandfather is playing at.'

Ezzy began to push the wheelchair along the uneven pathway, 'I am hurrying.'

'Maybe you should slow down then and be more careful,' Zam turned around and saw her looking at the mobile. 'Let me guess, you've broken a nail and need to make an appointment for a manicure?'

'I could leave you,' Ezzy said, frowning.

'Go on then,' Zam yelled, as he grabbed the wheels and began to push himself forward.

Ezzy stood, immobile, staring at Zam as he raced off, weaving a twisting path through the crowd of people making their way to the platform. Most of the pedestrians were too busy with their own concerns and hardly noticed the young boy in the wheelchair until he was right next to their legs, asking them to move out of his way or darting from gap to gap between one person and the next. When he reached the train he stopped. The platform was lower than the train floor. He couldn't get onto it alone.

Ezzy ran up to him out of breath. 'You nearly knocked that old man over. You need to look where you are going,' she gasped.

'Maybe I need some new eyes to go with my new tongue. Some different legs too.'

'Stop feeling sorry for yourself.'

Zam ignored Ezzy and pushed himself towards the train, pulling a wheelie when he reached it in an attempt to get into the carriage. It was too high, though, and his wheels smashed against the train, causing him to lurch over to the side, almost toppling him over his wheelchair.

'What's your problem today?' Ezzy asked.

Before Zam could answer, Rat jumped out of his pocket and raced down his right leg, onto the platform. Visibly shaking, the polecat sat up on its hind legs in front of Zam and stared at him quizzically.

Zam tightened his hands on the wheels, 'I'm sorry, Rat. I didn't mean to frighten you.'

Rat lifted his head as if acknowledging what Zam said. Then he raced up his leg, along his arm and came to a stop perched on Zam's shoulder.

Ezzy smiled. 'I'll go get the porter,' she said.

Zam watched his friend walk away from him. 'I don't know why she stays with me,' he said to Rat.

Rat curled into Zam's neck and closed his eyes.

Ezzy returned a short while later with a slight-looking porter who was carrying a ramp. The porter was breathing heavily and his red face looked strained. Ezzy offered to help, but he frowned and waved her away without a word of explanation. When he reached the train he began to unfold the ramp, positioning it between the platform and the doorway to the train's carriage. Satisfied the ramp was secure, he motioned Zam to enter the train with a nod of his head.

Ezzy took hold of the wheelchair handles and with Zam pushing on the wheels too, they eventually managed to board the train between them.

'What's his problem?' Zam asked, as they watched the porter drag the ramp back to its storage area rather than carry it.

'I think it's a boy thing. They all seem moody today.'

Zam was about to apologise for the way he had reacted earlier, when he saw Ezzy smiling at him. He returned the smile and remained silent.

The train was jam-packed with passengers and the only space available was in the lobby between carriages. Zam positioned himself next to the door. He hated the feeling of being enclosed and always tried to get a seat near a window or doorway.

'It must be something to do with the moon,' he said.

'What do you mean?' Ezzy asked.

'Boys and their moody behaviour today.'

The train started to pull out of the station and Ezzy leaned against Zam's wheelchair, 'What has the moon got to do with boys?'

'Boys are part werewolf of course. When there's a full moon it affects us in certain ways.'

'What, you go all hairy and moody?'

'No, we grow fangs and go all moody,' he said, grabbing her arm and pretending to bite it.

Ezzy laughed, pulling her arm from his grasp. 'You're crazy, Zam.'

'I don't want to go back to school next week,' Zam suddenly blurted.

'Me neither.'

'No, I mean I really don't want to go back.'

'School isn't so bad and we only have one year left, then we'll be sixteen. Then we'll be adults.'

'You don't know what it's like, you aren't called Napoleon Xylophone. You don't know what it's like not being able to walk more than a few steps before your legs give up and turn to jelly.'

'Yeah, and I'm not a lion of the woodlands either.'

'What do you mean?'

'Your name, Napoleon, its Greek meaning is Lion of the Woodlands. I Googled it on my mobile.'

'I don't feel like a lion.'

'You don't have to feel like something to be it. You have to think like it.'

'Oh yeah. I suddenly start thinking like a lion and everyone stops bullying me.'

'Have you ever tried thinking like a lion?'

'No, but I've tried thinking like a werewolf.'

'Yeah, but that only makes you grumpy.'

'Being in a wheelchair makes me grumpy.'

'I won't talk to you if you start feeling sorry for yourself again.'

Zam paused before asking the next question: 'Have

you ever tried thinking like a girl?'

'I am a girl.'

'You don't act like one. Girls are supposed to be sympathetic.'

'I can do sympathy when it's deserved.'

'Like I said, you don't know what it's like being in a wheelchair.'

'And you don't know what it's like being blind or deaf or... I don't know, to have two heads.' She stared into his eyes, looking for a suitable response.

Zam blushed and turned away from her, staring out of the window. 'I wish you'd stop thinking like a girl,' he said, watching Durham Cathedral pass by outside.

'Anyway, ' Ezzy continued, 'you have to go to school and then university or you'll never be an astronaut. You'll never get to visit Titan.'

'I'll never be an astronaut anyway.' Since watching Professor Brian Cox, the physicist, on TV talking about methane rain and how it falls in slow motion on Titan, he wanted to visit Saturn's largest moon more than any other place in the universe.

'You don't know that.'

Zam didn't know a lot of things. One thing he knew for sure, he would never see rain falling on Titan. Closing his eyes, he tried to imagine what it would be like to be blind.

He didn't like what he didn't see.

3

The train stopped at Newcastle and they waited for everyone to get off before waiting for a porter to get a ramp, then finally getting off themselves. Zam let Ezzy wheel him out of the station, knowing she liked to feel like she was helping. He stared at Ezzy's reflection in the long shop windows as she wheeled him along. As usual she was also staring at her reflection. One time, he had caught her looking at herself in a small, shiny doorknob. He asked her what she was doing and she said she thought she had a fly in her eye. *'The only thing that's ever in your eyes is your face,'* Zam said.

Zam rarely looked at himself.

A short walk later they arrived at their destination. Seeing the building on Grey Street where Zam and Ezzy stopped, most people would assume the three floors above the bank were offices belonging to the bank, but they would be wrong. All three floors belonged to Zam's grandfather – Eli Xylophone, along with the rest of the building and the bank.

Zam typed the key code into the panel bolted on the wall and then placed his finger on the recognition unit. A moment later the inconspicuous door at the side of the building silently swung inwards. They entered the doorway into a narrow lobby with a black, marble floor and plain white walls which led to an ancient-looking elevator with collapsible metal doors.

'What's that smell?' Ezzy asked as they walked up to the elevator.

'I don't know,' Zam replied. 'Do you think Grandfather has been cooking again?'

'If he has, I won't be eating with you tonight. It smells like something has died and then been sprayed with skunk juice.' Ezzy pulled the elevator doors to the side and stepped into it.

Zam followed her, always thankful it was such a large elevator, and placed his fingertip on the identification panel, waiting for it to bleep and flash green before pressing the button marked X. The elevator slowly creaked its way up and when it eventually came to a shuddering halt, Ezzy opened the doors and Zam wheeled himself directly from the elevator into the apartment where he lived with his grandfather.

Although his grandfather called their home an apartment, it was more the size of a small supermarket. Most of the internal walls had been removed to leave one central space with high ceilings and large, Georgian windows to the left and right. It had been furnished with the eye of someone who had no idea about furnishing. Expensive leather rocket chairs were placed next to the cheapest swivel office seats, while a large American-style freezer had been positioned next to a stuffed grizzly bear, and a rectangular fish tank sat precariously on top of an old dishwasher. Clockwork components were scattered around the space alongside half-assembled legs, arms, bodies and heads of robots. Grandfather's steam generator gently hissed in the background from the leak he had unsuccessfully tried to fix this past week. Apart from that and the unsynchronised tick and tock of his carefully selected Victorian clocks, there were no other sounds.

As soon as Zam entered the apartment he knew something was wrong. The door at the far end of the apartment that was always locked, gaped wide open. Zam had never seen the door open before and every time he had asked his grandfather what was behind the door, he always got the same answer: *"Don't ask questions about things that don't concern you."*

Zam had tried on numerous occasions to open the door when his grandfather wasn't in the apartment but failed every time. The door didn't appear to have any kind of lock, either mechanical or electronic. It didn't even have a handle.

He quickly wheeled himself towards the door and Ezzy followed close behind.

'What's wrong?' she asked.

'The door that doesn't concern me: it's open. It's never open.'

'That's where the smell is coming from, it's getting worse,' Ezzy said, covering her nose with her hand.

At the entrance Zam paused, almost too frightened to enter now that he finally could. Looking at the door, he saw it was as thick as his arm was long and the wall either side of the door was even thicker. No wonder he never heard any sounds coming from the other side of the door; it had to be soundproof as well as bombproof.

He peered inside.

The space was vast, larger than the apartment; so big it must have encompassed the adjoining building. There were workbenches and machinery and computers all lined up in perfect symmetry, like a factory designed for robots who liked everything to be in its correct and proper place. In the centre of the space Zam saw something that made him squint, just to make sure what he thought he saw was actually what he saw.

It was a wheelchair that didn't look like a wheelchair. It looked like the coolest vehicle Zam had ever seen in his life. Ignoring his unease, he pushed himself over to the platform where the wheelchair sat and slowly circled it.

'Wow...' he breathed.

Zam was impressed with the way his grandfather had incorporated steampunk influences into the wheelchair's build. The matt black frame was curvaceous with smooth lines and small, intricate fastenings a dull golden colour. The velvet-covered seat looked as if it had been moulded to fit a particular sized person and Zam hoped he was that person. It had two chunky wheels at the side designed for off road manoeuvres that were also rimmed, allowing the passenger to manually propel the wheelchair. Zam wondered if the material they were made from really was gold. Knowing his grandfather, Zam guessed he would have wanted to use real gold, but his sensible head would have gotten the better of him and he would have manufactured them from a strong, light alloy that was merely painted gold. Grandfather was particular about using the right materials for the right job. The rear axle was attached to a drive mechanism and Zam guessed there must have been a concealed battery to power it. Two smaller wheels at the front made the wheelchair look like it was sat prone, ready for whatever dared come its way.

'I wish this was mine,' Zam said, thinking he could deal with whatever came his way if he owned a wheelchair like that.

Ezzy circled the wheelchair behind Zam, 'It looks like it could fly.'

'Knowing Grandfather, it probably can.'

'Why has he kept this place such a secret? And this wheelchair, imagine what you could do with it. Why keep it from you?'

'You know what he's like. He doesn't trust himself. Doesn't trust his inventions, not since the accident.'

'But...' Ezzy started, then changed her mind.

'You're right about that smell. It is worse in here,' Zam

said, reluctantly turning away from the wheelchair and moving towards a control panel behind it. Something was dripping from the panel and when Zam got closer he saw a sickly, grease-like substance covering the panel and the floor beneath it. His focus didn't stay on the ooze for long though, not when he saw the specks of blood.

'Grandfather!' he yelled.

'Zam, what is it?' Ezzy said, joining him by the panel.

Zam pointed to the blood on the floor and when he saw Grandfather's phone, he wheeled himself around the workshop, speeding from machine to machine, looking under benches and behind control panels.

His grandfather was nowhere to be seen.

'I'm sure there's an explanation,' Ezzy said.

Zam quickly wheeled around, facing Ezzy, 'Of course there's an explanation.'

'I'm only trying to help.'

'You can help by finding Grandfather.'

'Please don't argue,' a voice called out from behind. 'I hate it when people argue.'

They both turned to where the sound of the unfamiliar voice came from, staring apprehensively from side to side, but they couldn't see anyone.

'Who's there? Come out where we can see you,' Zam said.

'Only if you promise not to argue.'

Ezzy stared at Zam. 'We promise not to argue,' she said.

After a moment, a shadow began to move across the wall towards them. Zam and Ezzy looked around, but they couldn't see anyone. The shadow suddenly stopped moving, dead still, as if they had been mistaken and it was really a silhouette painted on the wall. Just as swiftly, the shadow stepped off the wall and began to walk towards them.

'He took Eli away,' it said, standing in front of them like it was a perfectly natural thing for a shadow to do.

Zam wheeled around, looking for a projector or something else that could have made the shadow shaped like a man who now stood in front of them. 'Grandfather, this isn't funny. Where are you?' he yelled.

Ezzy stepped back, away from the shadow. Then she stepped forwards and hesitantly raised her hand, touching the shadow. She pulled away from it quickly. 'It's ice cold.'

Zam turned around and faced the shadow man. 'Where is Grandfather?'

'I already told you. He took him away.'

'Who took him away?'

'Mandrake Ackx.'

Zam's mind raced. He couldn't believe he was talking to a shadow. And Grandfather, where was he? Was this shadow man the reason he had warned Zam not to come home? Maybe they should leave and get away from the shadow or projection or whatever trick of the light it happened to be. But there was blood on the floor. It could be his grandfather's blood. Zam needed answers and right now there was only one place he could get them. 'Who is Mandrake Ackx and what does he want with my grandfather?'

The shadow began to waver, as if a wind had blown through it. 'You don't want to know.'

'Yes, I do want to know.'

'He's a wyte,' the shadow said flatly.

'What's a wyte?' Ezzy asked, wondering why one of the shadow's arms was tied in a knot.

'Can we talk about something else?' the shadow said, clapping its hands first in front of its chest then behind it's back.

'No,' Zam yelled, still not convinced this wasn't one of Grandfather's tricks. He stared at the blood on the floor. 'Tell me about this wyte. What is it and what did it want with Grandfather?'

'I can't remember. That happens to me a lot. Losing my memory I mean. Have I told you that before?'

Zam closed his eyes and began to rub his brow. *This can't be happening*, he thought. *I can't be talking to a shadow.*

'No, you haven't,' Ezzy said, wanting to ask about the arm tied in a knot, but deciding not to. 'What are you?' she eventually asked.

'I'm a shade.'

Ezzy leaned into the shade, squinting as she closely studied it. 'You're a ghost?'

'No, I'm a shade.'

'A shadow?' Zam said.

'No, a shade.'

'What's the difference?'

The shade sighed deeply, 'A shadow is just an image produced when light is blocked. It has no substance, no thought process.'

'But you look like a shadow,' Zam said, 'like someone is projecting you from an overhead projector.' He looked up above but could not see any signs of a projector.

'That's just the way it is.'

Ezzy looked up from her phone. 'A shade is a ghost,' she said, 'according to Wikipedia.'

'What's a ghost anyway?' the shade asked.

'You don't know what a ghost is?' Ezzy said, continuing to look at her phone. 'It's the spirit of someone who has died.'

'Eli told me I died.'

Zam touched the shade and pulled his hand away just as quickly as Ezzy had, when a funny sensation that felt like cold, but also like electricity, passed through his skin.

'What's your name?' Ezzy asked.

'I can't remember. Did I tell you I keep forgetting things? Especially when I'm upset.'

'I think we should call you Slink because of the way you slink in the shadows.' Ezzy said.

The shadow breathed in heavily. 'I'm not sure I like that name.'

'Okay, we'll call you Skulk then,' Zam said.

'Slink will do fine,' the shade said.

'What happened to Grandfather?' Zam asked impatiently.

'I'm trying to remember.'

'Why are you here and not wherever other spirits go?' Ezzy asked.

'I'm haunting Eli.'

'What?' Zam said.

'He killed me, so I'm haunting him.'

'That's a lie, Grandfather would never kill anyone.' Zam backed away from Slink and looked at him with new eyes.

'How did he kill you?' Ezzy asked.

'It was his invention. The one Mandrake wants him to work on again.'

Zam slumped in his seat. 'You're the reason Grandfather stopped working on his inventions? You're the accident?'

'He didn't stop working,' Ezzy said. 'Look around you at all the things he's made without you knowing.'

Zam's gaze followed Ezzy's hand gesture as she spoke, half taking in Grandfather's workshop, half taking in Ezzy.

'I've stopped haunting him now,' Slink continued. 'He's too nice to haunt. We talk a lot.'

'What do you talk about?' Ezzy asked.

'I can't remember.'

'Can't you remember anything that would help us?' Zam asked.

'Yes, yes, I can.'

'Well come on then, spill!'

'Oh, I'm sorry. I forgot what it is I was going to say.'

Zam lifted the front wheels of the wheelchair and smashed them on the floor. 'This is stupid.'

Rat popped his head out of his pocket and hissed at Slink.

Slink backed away from Zam.

'You have a changeling,' he said.

Zam looked down at Rat. 'It's okay boy, Slink is a... a friend.'

'A changeling?' Ezzy said.

'Ackx had a changeling with him. Changelings are unpredictable. You never know what they are thinking.'

'This is crazy,' Zam said. 'First a wyte, then a ghost, now a changeling. Are we in a dream or something? Please tell me this is just a dream.'

'Changelings stink when they are hurt.'

'Is that what that smell is?' Ezzy asked.

'Yes, it looks bloody awful doesn't it?'

Ezzy frowned. 'You mean it smells awful.'

'No, I always say what I mean.'

'How can you see a smell?'

'How can you smell a smell?'

'With her nose of course,' Zam said.

'And I can see smells with my eyes of course.'

'But, you haven't got any eyes,' Zam said. 'You're just a shadow.'

Slink waver-walked towards Zam and bent into his face. Two spots of light like sunlight shining through a canopy of trees suddenly appeared. 'That's because I had them closed, of course.'

'What does a smell look like?' Ezzy quickly asked.

'It depends on what's making the smell. A lily's scent looks like a spiral of multi-coloured light, but other flowers look different. I always liked lilies.'

'What does a changeling's smell look like?' Zam asked, almost not wanting to ask.

Slink shivered, 'This particular changeling's smell is like black smoke rising from smouldering rubber tyres. There is something more though, something I don't recognise. Like the hint of an aromatic flower I've never come across before. It's odd; usually stuff smells either black or white. This is the first time I've seen anything that has a nice smell as well as a bad smell.'

Suddenly excited, Zam tried to tug on Slink's arm, but his hand went straight through the shade. 'If you can see the smell, can you see where it goes?' he asked.

'Yes. The trail leads through that door.' Slink pointed to where they had come in.

Rat hissed one more time at Slink then disappeared back into Zam's jacket pocket.

'Can you follow the trail and lead us to Ackx and Grandfather?'

'Who is Ackx?' Slink asked, with his shadowy features crumpling into what Zam guessed to be a confused frown.

'I can see this is going to be frustrating,' Zam said to Ezzy, 'but he's our only hope of finding Grandfather.'

'What if the changeling's scent disappears as soon as we leave the building?' Ezzy asked. 'We could only smell it when we entered the main hallway.'

'What other choice have we got?'

Ezzy shrugged her shoulders and pulled the funny face that always made Zam smile. 'I suppose we had better get going then.'

'Yeah, but only after I change wheelchairs,' Zam said, moving towards the platform and the high-tech wheelchair. 'I have a feeling there is more to Grandfather's wheelchair than just good looks.'

Ezzy climbed the platform and looked at the wheelchair, searching for handles she could use to push it, but there didn't appear to be any attached.

'Hurry up,' Zam said.

'There aren't any handles.'

'Maybe Grandfather hasn't finished it yet. It doesn't matter; it's too cool to leave behind. Just push it by the top of the seat.'

Ezzy went to do as Zam asked, but quickly pulled away from the wheelchair when she touched it and it began to speak.

'Esmeralda Riley,' it said. 'Fifteen year old girl. Best friend of Napoleon Xylophone. Five feet three inches tall. Dark hair, green eyes. Ninety five pounds. Acceptable weight for human's current age and height, but she has a tendency to put on excess weight due to her addiction to M&M's.'

'I'm not addicted to M&M's.'

'It can speak!' Zam said.

'Prototype Q is installed with both a voice recognition unit and a speech communicator. As well as having access to a range of databases detailing anything from psychological reports on people of interest to Eli Xylophone to recipes for butterfly cakes.'

'You sound like Dr Who,' Ezzy said.

'Prototype Q is also installed with software that can emulate all recorded voices on planet Earth.' His voice began to change as he mimicked the voices of all the names he spoke out loud, 'David Beckham, Nicole Kidman, Albert Einstein, Marilyn Monroe, George Clooney, Lady Gaga.'

Then the wheelchair began to sing in a bad way. ' Ra-Ra, Ah-Ah-Ah, Ruma-Ruma Ah-Ah-Ah. Ga-Ga, Uh-La-La.'

'I think they get the point, Q,' Slink said.

'What does your own voice sound like?' Ezzy asked.

'I don't have a voice of my own.'

Zam wheeled himself closer to the platform, 'What's your favourite voice then?'

'K9,' the wheelchair said, in the voice of K9 from *Dr Who*.

'That sounds too… metallic. Choose another voice.'

'What about this voice?' He asked in the voice of C-3PO from *Star Wars*.

'Do you like the sound of any voices other than robots?'

There was a pause before Q spoke again. 'I like the way

Clint Eastwood sounds,' he said, in Clint Eastwood's voice.

'Cool,' Ezzy said.

'What else can you do other than talk?' Zam asked.

The wheelchair silently began to move forward, down the platform ramp, coming to a stop next to Zam. 'Napoleon Xylophone,' it continued in Clint's voice. 'Fifteen year old boy. Five feet five inches tall. Has a secret crush on Esmeralda Riley.'

Ezzy laughed.

'I do not,' Zam said, pulling a face that always made Ezzy smile.

Q ignored him, '105 pounds. Hates his name because other children call him Nappy. Changed his name to Zam which his grandfather hates. Diagnosed with Hereditary Spastic Paraplegia. He will never walk again.'

'Never say never,' Slink murmured. 'I can't remember who said that but I'm sure it was someone really important.'

'Just tell me what else you can do other than talk nonsense,' Zam said.

Q switched to Basil Fawlty's voice, 'One moment. Checking Napoleon Mode for inventory of functions. Inventory located. Functions include ability to scan environment, communicate with human life forms and transport Napoleon Xylophone to and from school.'

Zam looked disappointed, 'I thought there'd be more to you than talking and transporting. Are you sure you can't fly?'

'Negative. Flying is not on Napoleon Mode function list.'

'At least he looks cool,' Ezzy said.

'Yeah, I guess.' Zam unclipped the belt of his wheelchair and shuffled into Q's seat, which immediately seemed to mould into Zam's shape as he got into it. 'How are you powered, by battery?'

'Negative. My power source is a hydro-motive energy cell.'

'What's that supposed to be?'

'It's a type of battery.'

Zam buckled himself into Q. 'I see Grandfather programmed you with his crazy sense of humour.'

'Negative. Humour is a human function that always ends in trouble. I would never consciously use hilarity to express myself.'

'Being funny is a good way to get to know people,' Ezzy said.

Q popped a reverse wheelie with the rear wheel airborne and the front wheels fixed to the ground. Zam lurched forwards and then fell back into the seat when Q dropped the rear wheel back onto the floor.

'What was that all about?' Zam asked.

'I was being funny,' Q said, 'trying to get to know you better.'

'You remind me of Grandfather, are you sure he isn't somewhere around, making you do this?'

'Negative. Eli Xylophone has left the building,' Q said in a perfect Elvis voice.

Zam suddenly looked thoughtful. 'No, Grandfather

isn't here and it's time we found out where he is and what's happened to him.' He looked at Slink. 'We need you to lead the way. Why are your eyes closed?'

'They are?' Slink said, opening his eyes. 'I must find a way of remembering how to keep them open.'

Zam looked at Ezzy and was about to say something, but changed his mind. 'How do I get you to move?' he asked Q.

'Just tell me where you want me to take you and I will,' Q said, as a whirring sound came from his armrest and a joystick began to rise from it. 'Alternatively, you can use this to guide me where you want to go.'

Zam smiled. 'The more I find out about you, wheelchair, the more I like you. And I never realised it before today, but I've always wanted to say this: Q, follow that shade.'

With Slink in the lead, they followed him out of the workshop, heading for the elevator and Newcastle's soon to be discovered underworld.

Smaller than a child's hand, the Tarsier monkey remained unseen in the goldfish bowl as Zam and the others passed by on their way to the elevator. Slowly licking the rounded pads on its long fingers, it seemed unconcerned by them until they entered the elevator and the doors closed. Then it looked up and its large, disproportionate eyes started to glisten as if it was about to weep. It did not weep though; instead, it moved to the edge of the goldfish bowl and then jumped three meters into the air before landing softly on a Kodak Box Brownie camera, which had a flash attached to it that was larger than both the camera and the monkey. The Tarsier jumped again, this time landing on a metronome that fell over just as the monkey jumped one final time, landing on the ledge of an open window.

Tarsier monkeys do not have black fur, but this monkey's fur was as black as Mandrake Ackx's eyes and when it morphed into a crow, its feathers and talons and beak were just as black, just as light consuming. Only the creature's eyes were a different colour. Its brown eyes reflected light, rather than consuming it, and the crow stared outside without blinking as if it was reluctant to leave the building. Bending down low, the crow eventually skipped beneath the underside of the sash and once at the other side it stepped off the ledge and free fell without opening its wings towards the ground below. Just as it looked like the crow was about to be splattered against the pavement, it spread its wings wide and the updraft immediately lifted it high into the air.

The crow circled the area for a short time before finally settling on top of a lamppost opposite the doorway leading to Eli Xylophone's apartment. Almost as soon as it landed there, another crow set down beside it and began to preen the first crow's soft breast feathers. The crow lifted its head as it allowed its companion to continue preening, while it fixed its eyes on the doorway and waited for Napoleon Xylophone to exit.

Zam couldn't smell the changeling once they were outside, but it didn't matter; Slink could still see its trail. 'We have to do something about you, Slink,' Zam said. 'We can't make our way through Newcastle with a shade walking along beside us.'

'Don't worry about me. I'm good at blending in,' Slink said, as he melted into the ground and morphed into the exact shape of Ezzy's shadow. 'See, now I'm just like you, Ezzy.'

Ezzy moved from side to side and Slink moved perfectly in line with her shadow. 'This feels weird,' she said. 'Do all shades do this kind of thing?'

'I don't know. I've never spoken to another shade before.'

'Which way from here?' Zam asked impatiently.

'Keep going straight ahead and I'll tell you when to make a turn.'

'How did Ackx get through Newcastle without

attracting attention?' Ezzy asked.

Zam thought for a moment before speaking, 'maybe they were in a car.'

'They could be miles away by now if they were. We'll never catch them on foot.'

'I don't want to think about that,' Zam said. 'Q, you heard Slink, keep going straight ahead.'

Zam could almost appreciate how smoothly Q's wheels glided over the uneven footpath as they made their way down Dean Street, but his mind was full of his grandfather, wondering why a creature like Ackx wanted him. He couldn't believe how the day had turned out and still thought it was probably some kind of dream or a mass hallucination. If ghosts and changelings and wytes – whatever a wyte was – really did exist, he wondered what else lived just out of sight of normal people's view. Demons? Bogeymen? Fairies?

What if there really were zombie flesh eaters? How did they keep out of sight and how much flesh did they need to eat each day? Maybe he needed a gun and a stake and silver bullets or holy water.

Maybe it was time he stopped thinking.

He looked at Ezzy who walked ahead, guided by Slink's directions, and suddenly remembered Q's words earlier. He liked Ezzy a lot, but Q was wrong, he didn't have a crush on her, and even if he did, he was in a wheelchair and she wasn't. She had perfect legs and he tried not to look at them, like he always seemed to be doing lately. He was sure it had something to do with him not wanting to be disabled, wanting to be just like other kids; a normal kid. At least, that's what he told himself as he continued to stare at Ezzy's legs and her long dark hair. He liked that, too, and the way she laughed at his jokes, how her face changed and her eyes. That was it; he just liked to make her smile. He absolutely did not have a crush on his best friend.

Ezzy turned around and smiled at him, like she knew what he was thinking. He flashed her a quick smile then put his serious face on, wishing more than ever that he wasn't disabled.

As they made their way through the crowded streets, Zam attracted the usual stares from people who walked by. Ordinarily, this annoyed him, the fact they saw Zam as something worthy of staring at, like he was some kind of circus freak, different from them. Didn't they realise everyone was a freak? It was just that he was a freak in a wheelchair and they weren't. Today was different, though. Today he told himself that everyone wasn't looking at him; they were looking at his super cool wheelchair, envious that he rode in it instead of them.

That thought made him smile and then he stared at Ezzy again, unsurprised that she was staring at her own reflection in the shop windows they passed, while pressing the keys on her mobile. Pretty soon, he knew she would walk into someone or a lamppost. She was always doing that, but it never stopped her looking at herself whenever the opportunity presented itself. And he could perfectly understand why she always wanted to look at her face. He always wanted to look at her face too. Seeing her pressing buttons on her mobile phone was what he could never understand; the reason her phone was so important to her, how she had so many friends she needed to keep in constant touch with. He hated her friends, how they always kept her away from him, but he liked the way she smiled at her phone from time to time. He always liked to see her smile no matter where it was directed.

At Dog Bank, they turned right into Broad Chare and headed towards the Quayside. After ten minutes of following the pathway beside the Tyne without Slink uttering another word, Zam became anxious. 'Slink, can you still see the changeling's trail?'

'What changeling?' Slink asked.

Zam grabbed Q's wheels and pushed himself towards Ezzy's shadow. When he was on top of the shadow he began to pop wheelies, bouncing up and down on the pavement.

'You stupid, stupid shade, can't you do anything right?'

'What... what have I done wrong?' Slink said. 'By the way, you can't hurt me doing that you know.'

Ezzy began to laugh, but seeing the look on Zam's face she stopped. 'I'm sorry,' she said.

Zam's grip on the wheels tightened, then relaxed, then he began to laugh too.

'This is crazy,' Ezzy said, laughing again. 'How did we get ourselves involved with a forgetful ghost?'

'How did I get myself involved with a mad wheelchair boy?' Slink said.

'Listen Zam,' Ezzy said, 'maybe we should just call the police.'

Zam sighed. 'And then what? Tell them Grandfather has been abducted by a wyte with a pet changeling? Oh and by the way, there was a witness, a shade called Slink who used to haunt him until they became friends.'

'What about your parents?' Ezzy asked hesitantly.

'You know what they are like. By the time they answer my email it'll be next year. Anyway, they are out of the country again.'

Ezzy flicked her hair behind her ear and Zam's heartbeat quickened.

'Have we lost the changeling's trail, Slink?' Ezzy asked.

'The changeling's trail? Of course, the changeling's trail! No, I can still see it, but it's becoming fainter. I don't think it's going to remain around for much longer.'

'Please, Slink,' Zam said. 'Stay focused. You're my only hope of helping Grandfather.'

'Yes, of course. Stay focused. What makes you think I'm not focused?'

'Just tell us which way we need to go!'

'Ahead of course. In the same direction the trail leads.'

Ezzy walked beside Zam as they continued to follow the path alongside the murky-watered Tyne. 'I'm sure everything is going to be fine,' she said. 'Your grandfather can look after himself.'

'Yeah, I'm sure you're right,' Zam said, feeling sure she was wrong. He looked ahead and couldn't believe what he saw. 'Over here,' he said, indicating for them to stand behind a van illegally parked on double yellow lines.

'What is it? What's wrong?' Ezzy asked.

'We just need to stay here a few minutes,' Zam snapped.

Ezzy looked across to where Zam was staring. 'Oh,' she said, seeing Jenson Murgo and Richie Walsh walking towards them on the other side of the road.

Zam remained silent, but inside his head he kept repeating – xyz, xyz, xyz. Whenever he saw Murgo, whenever he was bullied, xyz comforted him. He was certain those three letters were significant. The only thing his mother had ever told him about his childhood was how he never spoke a first word when he first talked; instead, he spoke those three letters. They had some kind of meaning in his life that he had not yet discovered. He was also certain that when he did learn their significance everything was going to be good, everything was going to be bad.

He watched the two youths draw level with the van and then continue on their way in the opposite direction. They were playing nark-slap and Murgo, the taller one, was easily avoiding Walsh's blows as he bobbed up and down and from side to side like a brutish ballet dancer.

In the meantime he seemed able to slap his friend's ears at will, like his hands were guided missiles. And each time he connected, his laugh sounded so loud it drowned out the noise of the traffic.

When the distance between the youths and themselves grew large enough, Zam silently pulled away from the van without looking at Ezzy and they continued to make their way along the quayside.

Xyz, xyz, xyz.

6

'There's Grandfather's car,' Zam shouted as they neared Horatio Street and he saw the Mercedes 170S crookedly parked at the side of the road. Q pulled up alongside the car and Zam pressed his thumb into the fingerprint recognition unit on the driver's door handle. After he heard the familiar beep, he opened the door and noticed a folded note on the seat. He picked it up and read it out loud:

Napoleon,

I am perfectly fine. Please do not follow me any further. I will return to the apartment in a few weeks' time.

I am sorry I will not be there for you when you start school next week. Contact your mother and she will arrange for someone to care for you while I am away.

Please look after Q and try not to get too annoyed with Benjamin.

Keep well, Grandfather Eli

'How did your grandfather know you'd find his car?' Ezzy asked when Zam finished reading out the note.

'I'm not sure.'

'Why would he think you'd get annoyed with me?' Slink asked.

'I had a feeling you were Benjamin,' Zam said.

'Maybe it has something to do with Q,' Ezzy said, 'He obviously left the door to his workshop open so you'd find him.'

'But he told me not to go home, why would he think I'd find Q?'

'Since when have you ever done what you've been told to do?'

Zam scratched his chin.

'You look like your grandfather when you do that,' Ezzy said, smiling.

Zam smiled back, then suddenly had a thought. 'Q, have you got any ideas why Grandfather would think I could find his car here?'

'Mr Xylophone's car is fitted with GPS,' Q said in his most laid back Clint Eastwood voice. 'I am fitted with software and a receiver that can track GPS, so it is obvious he would think that way.'

'What! Why didn't you tell us earlier?'

'You never asked.'

Slink extracted himself from Ezzy's shadow and stood upright. 'Benjamin, yes, now I remember. I'm not Slink, I'm Benjamin.'

'Sorry Benjamin, you'll always be Slink to me,' Ezzy smiled.

'Is Grandfather fitted with a GPS device too?' Zam asked Q.

'Negative.'

'Is there any other way you could find him that you haven't told us about?'

'Negative.'

'Your grandfather's note said not to follow him, what are you planning to do?' Ezzy asked.

'I'm planning on not getting annoyed with Slink and I'm going to continue searching for Grandfather, of course. What else do you expect me to do?'

'His note said he was fine.'

'There was blood at the apartment. He's trying to protect me from something he's not telling me about, that's all the more reason to help him.'

'Maybe it's time we really do call the police now. We could show them the note and abandoned car. They'd have to believe us then.'

Zam ignored Ezzy and grabbed hold of Q's wheels, turning around, looking for signs of where his grandfather and his kidnapper could have gone next. He was puzzled; they were in the middle of nowhere without any obvious place for them to have disappeared.

'I wonder why the changeling went through that door,' Slink said.

Zam spun around and faced Slink. 'You can still see the changeling's scent?'

'Yes.' Slink pointed towards the ground a few yards away. 'It leads towards that door over there.'

'What door? I can't see a door anywhere.'

Slink tutted and glided over towards the floor where he had been pointing. He bent down and when his hand touched the floor, a metal door appeared in the paving that looked like it might have been painted red a hundred years or so ago.

'How did you do that?'

'How did I do what?'

'Make...' Zam started to say, but changed his mind. 'Can you open it?'

'I'm not sure. I can see ghost doors, but I've never had a reason to open one before.' Slink moved to grab the handle but his hand went straight through it.

'A ghost door?'

'I don't know if that's what they are really called, I just made that up now,' Slink said, 'but it seems like a good name to me.'

Ezzy walked over to the door and twisted the handle, pulling on the door at the same time. It lifted up to reveal a black hole that looked like it belonged somewhere deep in space. 'What's that noise all about? It sounds like someone is trying to tune in a radio without much success.'

'That's white noise,' Slink said, 'and before you ask, I have no idea what white noise is.'

Zam wheeled himself over to the edge and peered into the hole. 'I can't see anything. It's like looking at a wall that's been painted black.'

'Maybe I can help,' Q said, as a whirring noise came from his armrests and two small headlights suddenly appeared. The lights clicked into life and their twin beams revealed twisting steps carved into the ground, leading deep into the earth below.

'Damn!' Zam whispered.

'What?' Ezzy asked.

'It's… Nothing.' Zam wasn't sure when he first became anxious of confined spaces. All he knew was that being in a small lift, a crowded train compartment or any place where there wasn't plenty of space around him, made him feel like he needed to kick his way out regardless of what he had to kick. 'I mean, how am I going to get down there in a wheelchair?'

'Maybe I can help,' Q said, as a louder whirring noise came from beneath him and he started to rise from the ground.

'I thought you couldn't fly!' Zam cried out.

'This isn't flying,' Q said, as he started to descend the steps leading into the earth below. 'This is hovering.'

'Coolest cool,' Ezzy said.

As soon as Zam entered the ghost door, the white noise ceased and he felt the chill air of the tunnel envelope him as Q glided down the steps. Somehow, he managed to resist the urge to kick out and drag himself back up the steps. The cold air helped, but mainly it was because he had become practiced at managing his illogical fear of cramped spaces. *Think of something else*, he told himself in the calmest voice he could muster. *Think of Grandfather, instead.*

Yes, that was it; he was doing this for Grandfather. He had to be alright for Grandfather's sake.

He couldn't always control the panic attacks. Not so long ago, when he was inside a taxi during the summer holidays on his way to wheelchair basketball, the situation had got the better of him. He was in the rear seat and the taxi's air conditioning had broken down. The driver wouldn't open the windows because he was listening to football on the radio and said he couldn't hear it for the traffic noise when the windows were down. Zam tried to stay calm, telling himself to think about something other than the lack of space, the heat, the feeling he was breathing through bricks rather than lungs. He couldn't keep calm though and at the moment Zam cracked, he didn't recognise himself; he began to kick the driver's seat and then punch him on the back of his head over and again. Worse, he started to shout obscenities he didn't even know he knew.

The driver was always wary of him after that and always did whatever Zam requested.

'I've just realised where we are,' Ezzy said, as she clambered down the steps behind Zam and almost ran into Q in her excitement. 'And I always knew you'd be able to fly, Q.'

'I can't fly,' Q said.

'You know where we are?' Zam asked.

Ezzy stared at her mobile, waiting impatiently for her Google search results.

'Yeah, I kinda know. I think this is one of the entrances to Victoria Tunnel. Although the walls were made from brick as far as I can remember.'

'What's Victoria Tunnel?'

Ezzy smiled as her search results came through, 'It's a subterranean wagonway built in the 1800s to transport coal wagons from the Spital Tongues colliery to riverside jetties on the Tyne. It's over two miles long. Parts of it have been converted into sewers, but others are open to the public.'

Zam started to feel anxious. 'Two miles long? How cramped does it get?'

'From what I can remember, it's the same size all the way through. Dad took me on a guided tour when I was younger...'

Zam wished he hadn't asked. 'Sorry...' he started. Ezzy's father died fighting in a war in another country. She had told Zam she saw his number on the TV afterwards when the news presenter talked about how brave he had been. He had been number thirty-three to die in the conflict. She hated number thirty-three. She hated her father for being so brave. Most of all, Zam thought, she hated not having him around.

'It's okay. I should talk about him more.'

Q stopped making the whirring noise when they reached the end of the stairway and he gently fell to the ground. The tunnel walls were rounded and looked like they were constructed from melted rock, as if a hot drill had bored its way through the earth. There was just enough room to stand side by side and a foot or so of space was between the top of Ezzy's head and the roof of the tunnel. If it remained like this and the temperature didn't increase, then Zam supposed he'd be okay. As long as he didn't think about how much earth there was between them and the surface.

A loud bang behind made them all jump and when they turned around they saw the doorway was no longer open.

'Slink, what happened?' Ezzy said. 'And where are you anyway?'

Slink moved from the shadows and into Q's headlights.

'It must have been the wind,' he said.

Ezzy ran back up the stairs, guided by Q's light. 'I can't see the ghost door,' she said when she reached the top. 'Slink, can you touch the door to make it appear again?'

'There is no ghost door on this side,' he said.

'What do you mean?' Zam asked, feeling the panic rise inside his stomach.

'I mean there is no door on this side; it's only present on the other side.'

'But can you make it appear if you touch it like you did outside?'

Slink shadow-walked up the stairs and stopped beside Ezzy. 'See,' he said as he touched the place where the door had been only moments earlier. This time the door didn't appear. 'Like I said, there is no door on this side.'

'That doesn't make sense,' Zam said.

'What has made sense about today?' Ezzy said, making her way back down the stairway. 'And the only thing that makes sense right now is finding another way out of this tunnel.'

Zam knew Ezzy was right, but still, he didn't want her to be right. He wanted to get out of the tunnel now – back through the ghost door that was no longer there. He almost convinced himself it was a lie and the door was just hiding. Instead, he started to manage the panic. *For Grandfather,* he said to himself, following Ezzy's long shadow as she started to walk ahead of them, searching for a way out by stepping deeper into the earth.

For Grandfather.

The crow stood on the ghost door, preventing anyone on the other side from opening or even seeing it. A murder of crows cawed all around, as if each individual crow was praising it for a deed well done. The crow ignored the din they made and cocked its head, listening for sounds on the other side of the door. Satisfied it was all right to move, the crow stepped back and the ghost door immediately appeared. The crow then began to unfold like a flower opening its petals at high speed and morphed into a wolf covered in stiff, black fur. The wolf stood up like a man on its hind legs, opened the ghost door and stepped into the tunnel, blending in perfectly with the darkness inside.

7

Zam felt Rat moving around and watched as he slid out of his pocket and jumped from his leg onto the tunnel floor. He then sniffed the air and started to run in that lopsided gait he had, past Ezzy as if the tunnel were his domain and it was his job to lead them.

The tunnel echoed with every sound they made as they journeyed deeper into its dark core. Zam hated the taste of the tunnel inside his mouth. It was awful, like he imagined soil burned in a furnace would taste and an earthy odour permeated the air, making him want to gag. He was more concerned about Slink, though, than the foul taste in his mouth or the disgusting air he was forced to breathe. His ghostly companion had dissolved into the shadows and remained silent, despite all the questions Zam asked him about ghost doors and other things they couldn't see that Slink could. Before he became distant, Slink told them he could no longer see the changeling's scent. The tunnel only stretched out in one direction in front of them, so it didn't matter and, guided by Q's light, they followed the seemingly never-ending tunnel, hopeful it would lead them to Grandfather and a way out.

'Shouldn't you switch off one of your lights to save energy?' Zam asked Q.

'Negative. Eli Xylophone's energy cell has a 4000-hour life when used constantly at full power levels.'

'That's amazing,' Ezzy said. 'Why doesn't Zam's Grandfather sell masses of them?'

'Each cell costs over five million pounds to produce. It is not economically viable to market on a mass scale. It is however, ideal for a product like me.'

'You are more than a product, Q. You're... part of our gang.'

'We are a gang?' Q said, mimicking Marlon Brando perfect gangster voice. 'Like a bunch of criminals? '

Ezzy laughed. 'No, not criminals. More like friends who look out for each other.'

'What is our gang called?' Q asked.

'The Misfits,' Zam said.

'No it isn't,' Ezzy said. 'We haven't got a name yet, we only formed a minute or so ago.'

Q's lights brightened, 'I have never been part of a gang or had any friends.'

'I'm glad you are our friend,' Ezzy said. 'Glad you are looking out for us.'

Zam only half listened to the conversation as he tried

to concentrate on the space ahead of them rather than his close proximity to the walls, floor and roof. If he let his mind wander and think about how far underground they were, he knew he would lose control.

Q started to talk in a ridiculous French accent. 'I have a mirror, Friend Ezzy.'

'What do you mean?' Ezzy said.

'A mirror, here, see?' As Q spoke, a steel rod whirred its way out of his armrest and disentangled itself into a robotic arm. A small circular mirror attached to the end of the arm sparkled in Q's lights. 'Would you like to look at yourself?'

Ezzy stopped walking and stared at Q. 'Why would I want to do that?'

'It's been quite a while since you last looked at yourself. I thought you might become fretful.'

Zam started to laugh, like he hadn't laughed in a long time. It felt good laughing that way.

'Did you put him up to this?' Ezzy asked.

'This has nothing to do with me,' Zam gasped, trying not to laugh.

Ezzy started to turn away from them, then changed her mind. 'I'm not a prima donna,' she said, walking over to Q and bending down to look at herself in the mirror. 'It's just that I don't like to think I ever look vacant.'

'Vacant?' Zam said.

'You know, uninterested in life.'

Zam stopped smiling. 'What are you talking about?'

Ezzy stood up and began to walk away from them. 'Nothing, it doesn't matter.'

Q's arm began to fold back into the steel rod and quickly disappeared into the armrest. 'Have I done something to offend you, Friend Ezzy?'

'I'm fine. Just leave me alone. And it's Ezzy, not Friend Ezzy.'

'I am no longer your friend?'

'Yes, you're my friend. Just stop calling me your friend.'

Q reverted back to his Clint Eastwood voice. 'Zam, can you help me out here partner?'

'It's a girl thing,' Zam said.

Q started to move forward, following Ezzy. 'A girl thing?'

'Yeah, girls. They think differently to werewolves.'

'It looks like they think differently to CPUs too,' Q said.

Encouraged by Q's response, Zam continued. 'That's right, there is no logic to them. They laugh in the face of common sense.'

Ezzy rounded on Zam. 'That's right, werewolves and CPUs are full of common sense and full of common nonsense too.'

'Is this where we respond or remain silent?' Q asked.

'Common sense tells me we should stay silent,' Zam said, staring at Ezzy, having never seen her look so angry. It filled him with a new sense of attraction. 'Slink, are you sure there are no more ghost doors?' he yelled. 'We've been walking along this tunnel for ages.' He had to stop thinking about Ezzy that way. She was too good for him.

'There are no doors but I can hear something,' Slink said from the shadows.

Zam waited for Slink to say more. When he didn't, Zam spoke again: 'What is it you can hear?'

'Someone running.'

'Where?'

'Behind us.'

Rat stood on his hind legs and hissed into the tunnel behind them.

Zam wheeled Q around and as his lights moved across the walls, Slink came into view. Zam stared past him and into the tunnel as far as Q's lights shone but he couldn't see anything. They waited a moment, silently listening for the sound only Slink could hear.

'It's a girl,' Ezzy suddenly whispered.

Zam cocked his head but still heard nothing. It wasn't until the girl began to yell that he heard anything.

'Where are you?' she shrieked as she came into view at the end of the lights' beams. 'Where are you?'

The girl was no more than eight years old and she wore a long white dress that looked like it belonged in the 1800s. Her translucent form drifted towards them as her cries echoed around the tunnel like leaves twisting in the breeze. The girl's heartache was palpable and it made Zam feel so emotional he almost wept with her. When she reached them she didn't stop and before Zam could move out of her way, she passed straight through him. At the same time, a melancholic chill tingled its way down Zam's spine.

'That's the first shade I've ever seen before,' Slink said as they turned around and watched the girl disappear into the tunnel ahead.

'Did you feel how cold she was?' Zam asked.

'Negative,' Q said.

Zam turned towards Slink, 'You called her a shade, but she isn't the same as you.'

'She is the same as me.'

'She doesn't look the same as you.'

'You don't look the same as Ezzy.'

Zam was pleased to see Ezzy smile and when she leaned into him and gently twisted his ear, Zam smiled too.

'What's she doing down here anyway?' Ezzy asked Slink.

Slink turned around and quickly started to make his way back up the tunnel in the opposite direction to the girl. 'You need to ask her that question yourself.'

'Where are you going?' Zam asked.

'Anywhere, as long as it's far away from that ghost. She scares me.'

Zam followed Slink along the tunnel. 'But she's a ghost. How can a ghost be frightened of another ghost?'

'I don't know. All I know is she gives me the creeps.'

Zam stopped wheeling. 'Don't leave us Slink, we need you. Grandfather needs you.'

'Am I part of your gang?' Slink asked, bowing his head.

Zam looked at Ezzy and she winked at him. 'Of course you are,' he said.

Slink turned around and glided back towards them. He stopped in front of Zam. 'I think she's down here because she never had a mother. Her mother left when she was a baby. She doesn't know why.'

'What about her father?' Zam asked.

'He never knew she was alive; her mother never told him.'

'How do you know all this, Slink?' Ezzy asked.

'I saw it when she touched me.'

They were silent for a moment before Zam spoke again. 'Did you hear that?'

'Hear what?' Ezzy asked.

'The little girl, she's crying.'

'I can't hear anything.'

'Me neither,' Slink said.

'Do you think we could talk to her?' Zam asked Slink. 'She might know where Grandfather is or how to get out of here.'

'I'm not sure. She feels... More lost than I have ever felt before.'

Zam thought for a moment before speaking. 'Let's at least try,' he said. 'Who knows, maybe we can help each other.'

8

The girl sat huddled further along the tunnel with her head buried in her arms. Zam told Q to stop a few feet away from her, unsure of what to do next. 'Hearing her crying makes me feel, I dunno...' Zam said in a choked voice. 'She sounds so unhappy.'

'I still can't hear anything,' Ezzy said.

Although Zam couldn't walk more than a few steps unaided, he unbuckled himself from Q and stood up, leaning against the wall. 'I think this is something I need to do alone,' he said as he shuffled across to the girl.

Sitting down beside her, he waited a moment before he spoke. 'I'm Zam,' he gently said. 'What's your name?'

The girl's head remained buried in her arms. 'That's a funny name,' she managed to say between sobs.

'My surname is Xylophone.'

The girl giggled, 'Zam Xylophone.'

Zam laughed too, 'Yeah, I'll probably be called Mr X when I grow up.'

The girl raised her head and stared at Zam. 'I'll never grow up.' Her translucent eyes held a rich blue hue that sparkled with tears and, despite the still air, her long, fair hair moved as if a gentle wind blew inside the tunnel. 'I'm dead you know,' she continued, studying Zam's face.

Zam held her gaze. 'Yeah, I know.'

She looked to the ground. 'I haven't got a mother.'

'Everyone has a mother, and a father too.'

'I can't find mine.'

'I don't think you'll find them down here.'

'My mother wasn't a good person,' the girl said, bending down and moving her finger backwards and forwards. A stone on the floor rolled back and forth in tandem with her finger movements, even though she wasn't touching the stone.

Zam stared at the stone. 'How do you know that?'

'A good person wouldn't leave her baby.'

'I don't know about your mother, but I think you are a good person,' Zam said, rolling a stone back and forth with his finger in synchronisation with the girl.

The girl looked up, 'Why do you think that?'

'Because you cry like a good person.' Zam stopped rolling the stone and stared at the girl. 'It makes me want to cry when I hear you cry.'

'You're funny,' she laughed.

Zam laughed too.

'I'm sorry for making you want to cry,' the girl said.

'It's okay.'

She stared at the floor. 'I can't remember how I died.'

'Maybe you are not supposed to remember.'

'Do you remember the day you were born?'

'No.'

'Me neither. Maybe we are not supposed to remember that either.'

Zam's legs began to stiffen and he stretched them out in front of himself. 'I wonder how our memory remembers to forget the things we are not supposed to remember?'

'Maybe it's tied a knot in its arm like your ghost over there.'

Zam looked over at Slink. 'I keep meaning to ask him why he's done that.' Zam smiled to himself. 'He's frightened of you.'

'He's not frightened of me. He's frightened of death, like every other ghost. I remind him he is dead.'

'Have you met many other ghosts?'

'Yes, but none of them can tell me where Mama is.'

'Why are you down here under the earth?' Zam asked, wondering why the girl wasn't haunting the house where she used to live.

'I woke up here after I died.'

'Have you ever tried to leave?'

'I think so, when I first awakened.'

'How long ago did you awaken?'

'I don't know. Every day feels the same. Like time isn't moving for me. I can't remember yesterday, or the day before. All I know is I need to find Mama.'

60

'I have a feeling she is thinking the same thing about you.'

'Then why doesn't she come and find me?'

'I don't know.' Zam suddenly had an idea. 'Maybe you are both looking in the wrong place.'

'Where else would we look for each other?'

Zam patted his leg as he thought about how to answer. Like the girl, his own mother had abandoned him; his father too. It wasn't anything to do with his disability; they simply shouldn't have had children. They were like children themselves – selfish children. He thought about Ezzy then, what it would be like if she ever left. He remembered the good times they had had together, away from school and bullies, when they visited Saltwell Park or took the train to Durham and checked out the cathedral, even when they simply had a coffee at Mulligan's in Newcastle city centre. Great times. Great places. 'Maybe you should look in the places that used to make you feel good.'

The girl started to pat her leg, copying Zam as if she too was thinking. Eventually, she smiled, 'I know one place that made me feel good.'

'Have you been there... Since you died I mean?'

'No, I haven't. And I don't know why I haven't.' The girl stood up and stared down at Zam. 'My name is Yelena by the way. Yelena Yurich.' She giggled. 'Maybe one day people will call me Mrs Y. Or even Mrs YY.'

Zam laughed. 'And I could be called Mr ZX.'

Yelena suddenly looked serious, 'Do you hear voices inside your head?'

'No.'

'I used to hear lots of voices, but I only listen to one voice now.'

'Is it your own voice you listen to now?'

Yelena bent down towards Zam and whispered into his ear, 'I only hear your voice now. I think it is important to only listen to one voice when there are lots of voices inside your head.' She touched the side of Zam's face with her white, gloved hand. 'Goodbye, Mr X. Thank you for helping me.' She stood upright then and turned away from Zam as she started to spiral-run down the tunnel, running on the floor, the walls and the ceiling.

A moment later she was gone and Zam no longer felt any sadness. He pulled himself up by the wall and hobbled back towards Q. 'Mrs YY,' he grinned. 'How could Slink ever be frightened of you?'

Zam buckled himself back into Q's seat and stared ahead at the tunnel as it stretched out before him like a never-ending rabbit hole. Q didn't need to be told to start moving and set off in the only direction open to them.

'How did you know what to say to the girl?' Ezzy asked Zam.

'What do you mean?'

'You set her free.'

'How do you know she's free?'

'I'm not sure; I guess it's an instinct thing. It just feels like she's not haunting this place anymore.'

Slink appeared on the wall by their side.

'She's right, Zam. I can't feel her presence like I could when we first entered the tunnel. I think she's left to find her home.'

'Why haven't you left to find your home, Slink?' Zam asked.

'This is my home. I have no other.'

Zam wanted to press Slink further, but the tone of his friend's voice stopped him from asking any more questions about it.

Ezzy placed her hand on Zam's shoulder, 'You never asked her to help us.'

Zam liked the weight of Ezzy's hand on his shoulder. Her warmth too. 'It didn't feel the right thing to do – asking her for help, I mean.'

Ezzy took her hand away, 'Do you think we'll ever get out of this tunnel? It feels like we've been down here for weeks.'

Zam's hand instinctively moved to where Ezzy's hand had rested moments ago and stayed there. 'Maybe we will sooner than you think,' he said, pointing ahead where the tunnel began to split in two different directions.

Ezzy's face brightened and she ran towards the intersection. When she got there her mood changed. 'Both tunnels are identical,' she said, 'and it looks like both of them run on for miles.'

'What about the third tunnel?' Slink said.

'What third tunnel?' Ezzy asked.

'There, a few feet in on the left-hand side tunnel.'

Ezzy stepped into the tunnel and immediately spotted what Slink had seen. It was more like a small hole than a tunnel. She bent down and saw one of the white gloves Yelena had been wearing. Smiling, she went to pick the glove up, but as soon as she touched it the glove disappeared. 'It looks like Yelena helped us anyway,' she said, before entering the hole and disappearing from view.

'Ezzy! Ezzy!' Zam shouted, but as he approached the hole and looked inside, there was no sign of Ezzy.

'I'm okay,' she echoed back. 'It leads to another tunnel, but this one has brick walls and there are electric lights. It must be part of the original Victoria Tunnel.'

'Come back.' Zam hated being separated from Ezzy and he didn't like the idea of having to make his way through the small hole himself.

Ezzy popped out of the hole a moment later. 'At least we know we have a way of getting back into Newcastle,' she said as she pulled herself out and stood up.

'Was there a phone signal in the other tunnel?' Zam asked.

'I don't know, I never thought to check.'

Zam could hardly believe Ezzy's response. It felt strange, seeing Ezzy unconcerned about not having her phone connected to the network. He was about to comment about it when he saw Slink move across the wall and disappear into the hole when he reached it.

'Where are you going?' Zam yelled.

'To investigate,' Slink's muffled voice replied.

Zam turned towards Ezzy. 'Now we have three choices, which path do you think we should take?' He hoped they wouldn't have to go down the small hole that was pretending to be a tunnel, but he had a feeling that was exactly where they were heading.

'Somehow I think we only have one choice,' Ezzy said. 'Yelena left one of her gloves by the hole.'

When Slink returned a short while later, Zam's anxiety increased.

'The changeling's scent is visible inside the hole,' he said. 'It must have brushed against the side of the wall when it crawled through and re-opened its wound.'

Ezzy suddenly had a thought: 'You might be able to get through the hole Zam, but I don't think Q will.'

'Don't worry about me,' Q said. 'I'm smaller than I appear.'

Ezzy looked unconvinced.

'There's a ghost door inside the tunnel at the other side of the hole,' Slink continued. 'A door like the one that brought us here. I think your grandfather is on the other side of the door. Mandrake Ackx too.'

'You never told us much about Ackx before,' Zam said, not wanting to think about the hole anymore. 'We need to know more about him now.'

Slink started to waver like a shadow cast by a flame in the wind and Zam thought he was going to disappear altogether before he said another word. But he didn't disappear. 'Ackx is ageless,' he began. 'A supernatural being who has the ability to get inside your mind and once inside he plants seeds. Seeds that take root and grow into nightmares.'

'How does he get inside your mind?'

'Through your eyes.'

Zam thought for a moment. 'What if we avoid looking into his eyes, will we be okay?'

'I think so, as long as you don't allow him to touch you. His touch is extremely painful.'

'Great, and if he sneezes on us we'll probably come out in pink spots and our hair will turn bright green, right?' Ezzy said.

Slink stopped wavering, 'I've never heard of that happening before, but I guess it's a possibility.'

Zam sighed, 'How do we hurt him? What are his weaknesses?'

'I don't know.'

'We could always stamp on his foot,' Ezzy said. 'Break his metatarsal and he'll be in agony. Just ask any footballer.'

Zam had a thought, 'Q, what do you know about wytes?'

'A wyte,' Q said in an enthusiastic David Attenborough voice, 'is a mythical creature of great notoriety who has been recorded throughout folklore in a variety of different cultures. Each lore is diverse in describing the creature, but they all agree a wyte is not a likeable or friendly being. Supernatural in nature, they are part changeling, part anything that will breed with them. No two wytes are the same, other than they all seem to have psychopathic tendencies and are incredibly difficult to kill.'

'How do we kill a creature like that?'

'You don't. Instead, you avoid it at all costs,' Q said.

Zam grunted and quickly began to unbuckle himself from Q, sliding from the seat onto the floor where he began to crawl towards the hole. 'I'm a Lion of the Wood,' he said. 'Lions of the Wood avoid nothing they fear. Lions of the Wood confront their fears with a grin on their face and their fingers crossed.' Despite his new-found courage, Zam couldn't help but close his eyes when he entered the hole and hoped with all his lion heart that it wasn't too long before he crawled out of the other side.

'Lions of the Wood,' Slink said, as he watched Zam disappear into the darkness. 'I like our new gang name. I like it a lot.'

In the cramped space, Zam could feel the floor, the walls, the roof. Everything felt like it was crushing him and everything felt like it was about to overwhelm him. When he felt Rat scurry over his hand, he concentrated his mind on his friend. He listened as Rat moved up ahead, as if his friend was once again leading the way for him, scouting for any signs of danger. He focused on the sounds Rat made instead of the close proximity of the walls and the crushing feeling they were about to cave in at any moment and bury him in soil, which he was forced to inhale right now when it became dislodged by his movements. He started to sweat as the effort of pulling himself along the narrow passage quickly tired him and when he opened his eyes and everything remained black, he began to panic and breathed heavily, taking in more of the soil. He coughed the soil out of his mouth and suddenly heard Rat coughing up ahead and then sneezing in that funny way he did. Zam laughed and the panic attack lost its strength. Closing his eyes once more, he thought about being an astronaut, weightless, suspended in space above Titan. Being weightless this way meant he could move like everyone else. He longed to be like everyone else, but he knew he never would be.

He'd never be like he needed to be for Ezzy.

When he eventually pulled himself out of the hole at the other side, he opened his eyes wide and gasped in the cool air of Victoria Tunnel like it was his last breath. Sitting on the floor with his back to the wall, he looked around, relieved to see that this tunnel was larger than the one he had just left. Its brick walls were arched and wagon tracks led off in both directions. The bare electric bulb to his right flickered like it was about to die at any moment and its wavering light made it seem like the walls were breathing in the same air as Zam.

A moment later he heard Q's motors and when the wheelchair shot out of the hole, it came to a halt in the middle of the walkway. Q had shape shifted into what looked like an elongated go-cart. Zam continued to watch as Q's motors began to whine and whirr and his shape changed back to the familiar form of a super-cool wheelchair.

Disturbed by the noises Q made, Rat jumped onto Zam and buried himself in the folds of his jacket.

'Are you sure you're not related to a Transformer?' Zam asked Q.

'Negative,' Q said, 'robotic wheelchairs don't have relatives.'

Ezzy crawled out of the hole a moment later and stood beside Q. 'He's amazing,' she said. 'I wish I had a Q too.'

'You only like me because I'm a scoundrel,' Q said in a perfect Han Solo voice, 'there aren't enough scoundrels in your life.'

Ezzy's bare legs were covered in soil and her normally perfectly straight hair was tussled. Zam smiled as he watched her trying to straighten it with her hands. 'I'll ask Grandfather to make you a Q after we've rescued him.'

'I'll hold you to that,' she said, suddenly shaking her head from side to side to remove soil from it. She laughed then. 'I must look terrible.'

'You look cool,' Zam said. 'In a dirty kind of way.'

Ezzy laughed. 'So I don't look vacant then?'

Zam crawled over to Q and hoisted himself into the wheelchair. 'You never look vacant. I don't know why you are so worried about being that way.'

Slink slid out of the hole and Zam immediately began to question him, worried about Grandfather once more. 'Where's the ghost door, Slink?' he said as he buckled himself into the seat.

Slink moved towards the wall opposite the hole and touched it. A wooden door with a rusty handle immediately appeared in the wall beneath his hand.

'What's that up there?' Ezzy asked, pointing past the doorway towards the opposite end of the tunnel.

Zam stared in the direction Ezzy was pointing, struggling to see what she saw. He finally noticed a bulky shape on the floor but couldn't make out what it was. He wheeled Q towards the shape and stopped as he reached it. 'Stay where you are, Ezzy,' he said. 'Don't come over here.'

It was too late, Ezzy had already reached him and now stood beside Zam. She stared down at the shape on the floor and saw a gorilla-like creature that clearly wasn't a gorilla. It was too big to be a gorilla for one thing and for another, the fur covering its muscular body was too metallic, it shimmered in Q's light. The beasts head had been hacked off and lay on the floor in the middle of the tunnel, staring up at them as if it was still alive. Its black eyes and gaping mouth made it look like it was frozen in an expression of pure terror and Zam wondered what the last thought going through its mind must have been.

'Ackx's changeling,' Slink said when he joined them.

'Who did this to it?' Ezzy asked.

'Ackx of course,' Slink replied, turning away from the beast.

'Why would he kill his own ally?'

'Ackx doesn't have any allies. He only has things that are useful to him and things that are not.'

Zam turned towards Ezzy looking slightly uncomfortable. 'I haven't got a plan other than to see what we find on the other side of the door.' He stared at the floor as he spoke the next words: 'It would probably be wise if you didn't follow me in there.'

Ezzy turned her back to Zam, walking over to the door. 'You're probably right,' she said. 'Then again, it would probably be wiser if you just followed me inside.' Before Zam could react, Ezzy pulled the door open and stepped through the doorway out of sight.

'Your friend makes a good Lion of the Wood,' Q said.

'Yeah, she does,' Zam replied as they followed Ezzy through the doorway. 'That's what worries me. She is too headstrong to be a Lion of the Wood.'

Hiding within Zam's shadow, Slink entered the room he didn't want to enter, thinking he would make a better Field Mouse of the Wood.

The wolf remained still and silent in the hole while the smell of the changeling's blood seeped into its awareness, tormenting it like only kin blood could. Yet it did not stir until they entered the ghost door and closed it behind them. Then the wolf sprang from the hole on all fours and raced towards the changeling's body. It skidded to a halt beside the lifeless form and simply stared down at it for a moment before pulling back its head and howling its lament, deep into the red bricked walls of Victoria Tunnel.

10

Eli Xylophone's mouth gaped when he saw Ezzy step out of the shadows. When he saw Zam wheel into the light, he almost dropped the scalpel he was holding. 'How on earth did you two find me here?' his voice echoed around the space.

Hearing Eli's voice, Rat disentangled himself from Zam and raced over towards him. When he reached him, the polecat leant into Eli, rubbing his neck up and down his leg.

Eli grinned as he bent down and started to stroke Rat.

'We had a little help from a ghost,' Zam replied.

'Benjamin?' Eli gasped, raising himself up from Rat.

Slink appeared from the shadows, 'Oh, err, hi, Eli. How are you doing?'

'I told you not to get involved with this.'

'You did?'

'Look at your arm, why do you think it's tied in a knot?'

Slink looked down at his arm, 'Oh, yeah. It was to remind me not to help Zam search for you when Mandrake Ackx took you away. I wondered why it was knotted. I guess I can unknot it now.'

This time Eli did drop the scalpel.

Zam looked around the cavern, scarcely believing how something so large remained undetected below the streets of Newcastle. St James' Park could easily fit into the space and it still wouldn't be full. He gazed upwards and saw a gloopy substance dripping from the ceiling, making the floor glisten in wetness. The cavern was partially illuminated by a globe-shaped lantern suspended in mid-air. It barely penetrated the space, casting more of a dull glow than a bright light. The outer walls of the cavern remained unseen, hidden in shadow, as if the creature that occupied this place preferred light that concealed more than it revealed. Despite its size, the cavern smelled dank and airless, like a cellar that hadn't been opened for centuries.

'Napoleon, are you listening to me?' Eli bellowed.

Zam jumped in his seat and stared at Eli. 'What's going on, Grandfather? Why are you here? And where is this Ackx?'

At the mention of Ackx, Eli visibly shrank, as if everything that made him alive had been sucked out of him. 'You have to leave now,' he said, 'before it's too late. All of you must leave.'

'That's a great idea,' Slink said, heading for the door. 'Let's leave right now.'

'I'm only leaving if you come too,' Zam said.

'I can't leave. I have to stay,' Eli said.

'Why?'

Eli looked down at the workbench. 'This is why,' he said, lifting up a chunk of flesh that looked like a jellyfish covered in slick, black oil.

'What is it?' Zam asked.

'That's the thing that killed me,' Slink said, before Eli could speak.

Zam wheeled himself over to his grandfather's side. 'Did you really kill Slink?' he asked.

Eli looked puzzled for a moment until he realised who Zam was talking about. 'Yes,' he eventually said.

'No you didn't,' Slink said. 'The Relater killed me. After Ackx forced me to put it on.'

'Put it on?' Zam said.

Slink glided over to the workbench, 'You wear it like a helmet, only it covers your face as well as your head.'

Zam stared at the black globule, which appeared to be moulding itself around Grandfather's hands as he continued to hold onto it. 'Why would you want to put that thing on your head?'

'To listen to Time speak. And to speak to Time yourself,' Eli replied.

Ezzy joined Zam at Eli's side. She poked the Relater with her finger and it disappeared into the black flesh. 'It feels freaky,' she said, quickly pulling her finger out of it.

'How does it let you to speak to Time?' Zam asked.

Eli dropped the Relater back onto the bench and it made a squelching sound as it landed. 'It connects with the neuron pathways in your brain and acts as a transmitter-receiver with Time.'

'But Time doesn't talk. Time isn't, I dunno, like a person.'

Eli picked up some small devices that were lying on the workbench and put them in his pocket. 'You are correct. Time isn't like a person, it is conscious, but more than conscious; it is everyone's awareness.'

'You mean we are part of Time?' Ezzy asked.

'Putting it nice and simple, Miss Riley, yes. We are all a part of Time,' Eli replied.

Zam scratched his head, 'I don't understand, if what you say about Time is true, how do you know it's true?'

'Mandrake taught me. He taught me everything.'

Ezzy checked her phone for a signal, wanting to Google Time. 'If he is so clever, why doesn't he just make the Relater himself? Why does he need you?' She wasn't surprised to see there was no signal.

'Because he isn't very good at making things. He's just good at coming up with ideas.'

Still curious, Ezzy pressed her finger into the Relater again, this time keeping it there. 'It tingles, like electricity,' she said. 'How did you make something like this? It almost feels alive.'

'It is alive,' Eli said.

Ezzy quickly pulled her finger out of the Relater, 'That's even freakier.'

'It's a new species of life bred for one specific reason. It's part tardigrade, part fungus and all supernatural.'

'What's a tardigrade?' Zam asked.

Eli looked around, as if he expected someone else to walk out of the shadows. 'A tardigrade is a microscopic animal with eight legs, commonly known as a moss piglet. It can withstand extreme temperatures, survive in a vacuum and live for a decade without the need for water. Mandrake said it would make an excellent foundation for the Relater.' Eli picked up the scalpel and began to cut into the Relater.

'What are you doing?' Zam gasped.

'Keeping it alive,' Eli said, and as he continued to cut into the Relater it began to give off a foul smell.

'How does cutting it keep it alive?'

'It hasn't got a way of releasing wind, so I have to cut it from time to time.'

'Wind?' Zam said.

'He means it can't fart,' Slink said. 'And before you ask, its scent looks like snot running down a bull's nose.'

Ezzy pulled away from the Relater. 'That's gross,' she moaned.

'It is highly flammable at the best of times,' Eli continued. 'I'd hate to think what it would be like if I didn't release all the gas it produces.'

'Did Time kill Slink or the Relater?' Zam asked.

Eli stared at Slink as he answered, 'I think it had a little to do with both. As soon as Mandrake put the device on Benjamin's head, he collapsed. When I removed the Relater from him, I saw he had aged incredibly fast. It was like he had gone from his true age of twenty-three to a man in his nineties in a matter of seconds.'

'I was overwhelmed,' Slink said. 'As soon as it covered my face I was simply overwhelmed. That's all I can remember.'

'What happened when Ackx used the Relater?' Zam asked.

'He hasn't used it yet. He's afraid it will age him too.'

'So he wants you to fix it so it doesn't age him?'

Before Eli could answer, a low guttural noise sounded behind them, like the final gasp of someone being strangled. When Zam looked past Grandfather, he was shocked to see what was making the noise and even more shocked he hadn't noticed the creature before

He knew instantly that he was staring at Mandrake Ackx.

Ackx was sitting upright with his eyes closed and his long skeletal legs bent at an impossible angle. The soles of his bare feet were pressed together and his thin arms dangled at his side without touching the floor as if his body was freakishly longer than his arms. Ackx's body wasn't longer though; his hands didn't touch the floor because of the way his shoulders were hunched up, like he had been in a car accident and his form had been mangled and misshapen with his neck pushed into his chest. His skin was incredibly white yet somehow his hair was whiter still and the loose, black suit he wore gave him the appearance of a perfect black and white creature. Beside him lay a walking cane which looked like the leg of some strange creature Zam didn't recognise. The white boned cane had a black hoof at the end of it, making it match Ackx's black and white persona exquisitely.

'Is that Ackx?' Ezzy asked.

'Of course it is,' Zam said.

Ezzy frowned, 'Why didn't we notice him before?'

'Because it's too late,' Slink answered, 'he's already got inside our heads.'

'What's wrong with him? Is he drugged or something?' Zam asked, staring at Ackx, feeling his stomach tighten as he did.

'He is listening to Time,' Eli said, keeping his eyes fixed on Zam, not wanting to look at Ackx.

'I thought he needed the Relater to listen to Time?'

'He has always had the ability to *listen* to Time. He only needs the Relater to *speak* to Time. Time does not hear a single word he speaks.'

Zam didn't want to stare at Ackx either, but he couldn't stop himself. 'How can he listen to Time?'

Eli followed Zam's gaze. 'He's different to us. He is a supernatural being. He sees and hears things we do not.'

'But Time... It isn't something that talks.'

Eli stepped in between Zam and Ackx, blocking his view of the wyte. 'Time is the narrator of life. Without Time speaking, nothing would exist.'

'You mean Time says everything that happens in our

lives and then it happens?' Ezzy asked. Like Eli, she couldn't look at Ackx for more than a brief moment.

Eli smiled despite himself. 'Simply put again, Miss Riley, yes, that is exactly what it does.'

'That's impossible,' Zam said. 'How can any one thing say everything that happens?'

Eli scratched his beard, 'You are thinking in terms of how you speak, when you need to be thinking in terms of how Time speaks.'

'So how does Time speak?'

'Through thought. Your thoughts, Ezzy's thoughts, even Benjamin and Q's thoughts. Everyone and everything that thinks is part of Time. Just like you are a collection of cells, Time is a collection of thoughts.'

'It feels like he is staring at me, even though his eyes are closed,' Ezzy said.

'Keep away from him, Ezzy,' Slink pleaded.

Scampering across to where Ezzy stood, Rat stopped beside her, arching his back. Biting on her shoe, he then started to pull at it, as if he was trying to drag her away from the wyte.

'Okay Rat, I get it,' Ezzy said, moving away from Ackx while attempting not to step on Rat.

Zam wheeled Q past his grandfather and started to circle Ackx as he spoke, both fascinated and fearful of the wyte at the same time. 'When you said Ackx is listening to Time, you mean he is listening to our thoughts?'

Eli kept his back to Ackx, staring at Ezzy as he spoke

to Zam. 'No, I meant what I said. He is listening to Time. Both future Time and Time past.'

'What about the present?'

'Time cannot speak in the present. Only the past and the future.'

'Is anyone else confused here?' Slink asked. 'And does anyone know why I have my arm tied in a knot?'

Zam didn't understand either, but he ignored Slink and continued to question Grandfather. 'Why does Ackx want to speak to Time?' He stopped directly in front of the wyte, staring at its face for a moment before quickly wheeling away as a shiver mischievously crept down his spine.

'He said Time is becoming weary of life. It wants to stop talking. If that happens then everything becomes nothing. Mandrake wants to offer Time another option. He wants to become Time himself.'

Zam couldn't see any movement from Ackx; it was as if he wasn't breathing, wasn't alive. Like he was frozen in time. 'How is he going to do that?'

'He intends to merge with Time and become nothing, become everything. Then he will speak in place of Time.'

'Is that possible?' Ezzy asked.

'Mandrake believes it to be so.'

'But Slink said that when Ackx gets into your mind, he turns your life into a nightmare,' Zam said, finally able to take his eyes away from Ackx and immediately feeling his spirit lift. 'If he becomes Time, he would make everything a nightmare.'

'Mandrake told me he wouldn't do that. If he did, then everything would collapse and it would be the same as letting Time stop talking.'

Zam wheeled himself over to Grandfather. 'Do you believe him?'

'No.'

'So you're not going to make the Relater safe for him to use.'

'I have no choice but to make it safe for him.'

'Why?'

Eli looked directly into Zam's eyes, 'If I don't, he said he is going to turn your life into a nightmare.'

Zam blinked then his eyes narrowed. 'If he becomes Time he'll make everyone's life a nightmare.'

'He said he wouldn't.'

'But you said you don't believe him.'

Eli grabbed hold of Q, pushing Zam away from Ackx and back towards the workbench. 'You need to leave now, before he wakes up.'

'I'm not leaving without you.'

'I can't escape from him.'

'None of us can escape from him now,' Slink said. 'It's too late.'

Zam shot Slink his angry eyes, 'We can at least try. We have a chance while he's sleeping or listening to Time, or whatever it is he's doing.'

'Where are we going to escape to?' Eli asked.

'Victoria Tunnel is at the other side of that door. It

leads back into Newcastle. From there we can go anywhere in the world.'

'What door?'

'The door we came through…' Zam turned towards the door, but even before he checked, he knew the door would no longer be there. 'Help me, Grandfather. There's got to be another way out of this place. You said I had to leave, how did you expect me to leave?'

Eli walked over to Ackx and looked down at him. 'He'll be in a rage when he discovers I am gone and he'll come looking for me again.' He turned towards Zam. 'I'll come with you, but only to make sure you are in a safe place. Then I'll have to return.'

Zam bit his lip. 'Can't you do something to him while he's asleep?'

'Kill him, you mean?' Eli said accusingly.

Zam blushed, 'Isn't that what he'd do to us?'

Eli's tone hardened. 'There are unnameable things far worse than death.'

'What about the police?' Ezzy said.

Eli turned towards Ezzy, 'We are dealing with the supernatural here. Haven't you understood that yet, Ezzy?'

'Yes, but…'

'I know, you are reverting back to normality to try and make sense out of things.'

Zam had heard enough. 'Let's just get out of here. Slink, can you see any other ghost doors?'

Slink stopped trying to untie the knot in his arm and moved towards Ackx, then thought better of it and swung around him, giving him a wide berth. He disappeared into the shadows and Zam began to wonder if he'd ever return. A moment later, he did.

'Follow me,' was all Slink said as he headed back into the shadows and disappeared.

Zam beckoned the others to quickly move and as they followed Slink, Q's lights revealed him waiting by the far wall. When he saw them, Slink touched the wall and two metal doors appeared. 'I don't know where this leads, but it's the only exit I could find.'

Zam wheeled himself over to the doors. 'If this is the only choice we have, then we have to take it.' He noticed a button beside the doors and when he pressed it, the doors slid open, revealing a small compartment with steel-clad walls inside.

'It looks like a lift,' Ezzy said.

Zam stepped inside, 'Come on, let's get out of here before that thing wakes up.'

Rat jumped onto Zam's lap and then darted into his jacket pocket. When the others entered the lift, Zam pressed the only button he could see and the doors slid shut before the lift began to move upwards.

The moment the doors closed, the changeling padded out from the shadows at the far end of the cavern where the ghost door was now visible again. No longer a wolf, it had taken on the form of a lioness, with fur as black as a starless galaxy. It walked towards Ackx and began to lick his face when it reached him.

'Thank you for bringing the boy to me,' Acxk said without opening his eyes.

'The boy brought himself,' the changeling replied.

Ackx's breathed heavily, 'What is wrong with you, child?'

'Why did you kill my brother?' the changeling asked.

'I do not know,' Ackx said in a hushed tone.

The changeling stopped licking Ackx's face and sat down, staring at him for a moment. 'You are becoming your father,' it eventually said.

'Yes,' Ackx replied, 'I think you are right. Does that alter anything?'

'Nothing you could understand,' the changeling said, as it stood up and began to walk back towards the ghost door leading to Victoria Tunnel.

'Where are you going?'

'To bury a warrior,' the changeling said before it disappeared through the ghost door.

Ackx opened his eyes and something like a smile crossed his face. Something like the smile a crocodile makes while eating its lunch. 'Hurry back,' he said, 'it will soon be time to bury another warrior.'

'This lift is totally out of place,' Ezzy said. 'I wonder where it takes us.'

Zam anxiously rocked back and forth. 'This whole day is totally out of place.'

The lift came to a halt and when the doors slid open, Zam quickly exited and found that it opened up into a small lobby. A discarded sign leaning crookedly against the wall read – *John Lewis Women's Underwear Department.*

'John Lewis,' Ezzy said. 'Why would a lift from Ackx's place lead to a department store?'

'The lift isn't there anymore,' Zam said.

Ezzy turned around and saw the steel doors had disappeared and been replaced with a flat painted wall. 'Oh, I guess that explains everything,' she said.

'Where do we go now?' Q asked.

'We can't go back to the apartment,' Zam said, 'Ackx will look there first. Grandfather, what do you think we should do now?'

Eli scratched his beard, 'I'm not sure. I was going to return to Mandrake in the lift, but now…'

Zam tapped his foot impatiently against Q's footrest. 'Stop worrying about Ackx. He's gone and so is the lift. We just need to find a place where he can't find us.'

Eli raised his eyebrows. 'You don't know Mandrake. He can find us anywhere.'

'How do you know that?'

'Because he listens to Time. He knows everything.'

'So what do we do, roll over and wait for him to come and get you?'

'Yes.'

'We are Lions of the Wood; we don't roll over for anyone unless it's to let them tickle our bellies,' Slink said.

'Well spoken, Slink,' Zam said, 'kinda.'

Ezzy tugged Eli's arm, 'You said Time talks about the past and the future and that Ackx can hear what Time says. Does that mean Ackx can look into the future to see where we are going?'

'I'm not sure. When Time speaks about the future, it annoys Ackx. He said the future keeps changing. He thinks our present actions aren't fixed; if we do things differently in the present, then the future he saw changes.'

'That makes total sense, not,' Zam said.

'I need to let mum know where I am,' Ezzy said, taking her phone out of her pocket before pressing some buttons. 'Great, there's no signal here either. What's wrong with the world today?'

Zam sat up from his slouched position. 'Can we go to your house Ezzy? Just until we work out what to do.'

'Yeah...' Ezzy hesitated. 'I guess. As long as Mum doesn't see Slink. I don't think she'd ever recover from seeing a ghost.'

Still attempting to unknot his arm, Slink didn't hear Ezzy.

'This isn't home,' Eli said, 'we are still in the underworld.'

Ezzy didn't even half listen to Eli's warning. 'I need to find Mum,' she said, heading for the main aisle, 'I need to know she is safe.'

'Okay, let's get going,' Zam said, indicating for Q to move forward. 'Once Ackx realises Grandfather is gone, he's sure to come looking for us.'

As they exited the small corridor into the main shopping floor, Zam immediately knew things weren't going to be as simple as going to Ezzy's house. The first mannequin they saw pushed a buggy while idly looking at the goods either side of the aisle, like it was a perfectly natural thing for a shop mannequin to do. It had no eyes or nose or mouth and its white face was smooth and hairless like a perfectly formed egg. The baby inside the buggy wasn't human either, it too was a mannequin, but it gurgled like a human baby would anyway, even though it too didn't have a mouth. Looking around the store, Zam saw that all of the shoppers moving around were mannequins. The humans in the store stood perfectly immobile in various poses, like mime artists impersonating mannequins.

'Are you seeing the same thing I'm seeing?' Ezzy said.

'Grandfather...' Zam started to say.

Eli placed his hand on Zam's shoulder. 'I think we need to get out of here right away.'

The mannequin pushing the baby looked up and saw them walking towards it. Its blank face remained unaltered and its mouth unseen, yet it began to wail like a fox screeching in the night as it raised its arm and pointed towards them. The other mannequins turned around one by one and when they saw Zam and the others, they followed the lead of the first mannequin and pointed at them before screeching in that awful way.

Without a single word needing to be said, they bolted along the aisle with Zam in the lead, heading for the main exit. Most shop doors were usually too heavy for Zam to easily open while wheeling his chair along at the same time, but today was different. As he approached the door and readied himself to lean into it, using his shoulder to wedge it open, he was taken by surprise when the robotic arm whirred out of Q's arm rest. Q directed the arm towards the door and pushed it open as they raced though the exit and into the main shopping thoroughfare outside. Zam was about to thank Q, when he saw all the people outside were frozen like the shoppers inside John Lewis. Some of them were in mid-step, some were motionlessly talking to one another while others were eating or had a mobile pressed to their ears.

'You were right, Grandfather. We aren't in Newcastle city centre,' Zam said, as the others bundled out of the store and stood around gaping at the strange world they now found themselves in.

Eli didn't answer. Instead, he stared at the deep red sky above as it shifted from cloudy to clear, like a film reel running at triple speed.

'Where are we then?' Ezzy asked.

'We're in Mandrake Ackx's world,' Slink said.

'Where is that exactly?'

'And how do we get back home?' Zam added.

'We're in the underworld,' Slink said.

'You mean we're in hell?' Ezzy asked.

'Not hell, not quite,' Eli answered. 'The underworld is a supernatural place. A place where all of those mythical creatures from the past are not so mythical. A place where Mandrake can mould and twist things to his own way of thinking.'

'Have you been here before?' Zam asked.

'Yes, I have. But this is different; this isn't the underworld as I remember it. I think Ackx is playing with our minds. One of our minds in particular.'

'What do you mean?'

'I think he's using the thoughts, the fears, of one of us to transform the underworld into what we now see.'

'He can do that?'

'Mandrake can do a lot of things. He is a powerful creature. More so than any other I have ever encountered.'

Zam still had a million questions he wanted to ask his grandfather. But he only asked one. 'How did you get involved with Ackx?'

Eli didn't get the chance to answer as the doors behind them burst open and mannequin after mannequin stepped out of the store, pointing at them and screeching. Before they could react, a mannequin dressed in a wedding gown grabbed one of Ezzy's arms, while another dressed in holiday shorts and a t-shirt grabbed her other arm and they began to pull at her like they wanted to split her in half. More of the mannequins pointed at Ezzy and screeched while others moved menacingly past her towards Zam and Eli, with their arms outstretched like they wanted to tear them apart too.

'Q, Combat Mode,' Eli yelled.

'Affirmative,' Q said, and in the voice of Winston Churchill he continued: 'We shall fight them on the beaches, we shall fight them in the air and we shall fight them in Newcastle city centre.'

'Get away from her,' Zam yelled, as he grabbed Q's wheels and attempted to push himself towards Ezzy. Q's wheels were locked though, and Zam couldn't push himself anywhere. He suddenly heard the familiar whirr of motors and then felt the vibration of shifting alloy as Q began to morph into a different kind of wheelchair. A wheelchair that no longer needed wheels. A wheelchair that could fly.

As Q left the ground and floated in mid-air, his wheels were roughly pulled from Zam's hands and they first shifted vertically downwards, then flipped 180 degrees before disappearing beneath Q's undercarriage. At the same time, Zam's legs were tightly bound into Q's seat when a number of metallic strips fastened themselves around his thighs.

'Use these to guide me where you want to go,' Q said, as two substantial joysticks appeared on his armrests. Without much thought other than to help Ezzy, Zam grabbed the joysticks and pushed them as far forward as they would go. Q instantly accelerated at great speed and smashed into the mannequin dressed in the wedding outfit, knocking it to the ground. Zam lurched first backwards then forwards, surprised how quickly Q could move and pleased to see the mannequin's head broken into plastic pieces on the floor. One of the mannequin's arms still held onto Ezzy, its hand refusing to let go and Ezzy wrenched the arm off and began to pound the other mannequin with it over the head.

Zam pulled back on the joysticks and Q came around as Zam guided him towards the mannequin dressed in summer shorts and propelled Q into it, knocking the mannequin off its feet. Ezzy stared open-mouthed at Zam as she watched him fly towards the remaining mannequins running from John Lewis' doorway and drove into them time and again, knocking them to the ground as legs and arms and heads lay scattered on the pavement. When all of the mannequins lay broken on the floor, Zam surveyed the plastic carnage and only then noticed how intense his breathing had become.

'Zam, look,' Ezzy said, pointing to the shops on the other side of the thoroughfare.

Zam stared in the direction where Ezzy pointed and saw more mannequins racing from the doorways of each and every shop around them.

There were too many of them.

'We have to get away from here!' Eli shouted.

Zam desperately looked around for a way for them to escape and noticed a number of cars at the end of the street.

'Down there!' he shouted, pointing at the cars.

Eli and Ezzy didn't need an explanation and they ran for the cars with Slink flickering in and out of view behind them. When they reached the cars, they tried to get into one, but the doors were locked.

'Q, can you help?' Zam yelled.

'Affirmative,' Q said in his best C-3P0 voice, as a variant of the robotic arm he had used earlier to open the store door shot out of his armrest and whirred its way in the direction of the ice cream van they stood next to. Q guided the arm towards the van door and a thin metallic strip extended from the arm then entered the door lock. The arm twisted in the lock and the door clicked open. Q's arm then entered the ice cream van, pushed the metallic strip into the ignition and a moment later the engine started.

'Get inside,' Zam shouted, as he watched the mannequins' rapid approach.

Eli and Ezzy scrambled inside the van and as Ezzy stumbled against the dashboard, her arm caught a switch and the theme tune from *The Magic Roundabout* blasted out from the Grampian Horns on the roof of the van.

Eli slammed the door shut as he sat in the driver's seat. 'Where to?' he asked Zam.

'I know we are not really in Newcastle, but Ezzy wants to go home,' Zam replied. 'Drive to her house and let's see what we find there. I'll follow on Q.'

Eli nodded, but didn't look convinced. 'Turn that music off, Ezzy,' he shouted.

Ezzy pressed all the switches she could see on the dashboard and the windscreen wipers began to move backwards and forwards. Then the windscreen wash squirted water and the heater started blowing wildly. *The Magic Roundabout* theme tune continued to blast out of the horn.

'Forget it,' Eli said as he popped the ice cream van into the wrong gear and the van jerked backwards.

In the back of the van Slink shook from side to side, but it didn't stop him from attempting, unsuccessfully, to pull an ice cream from the dispenser. 'Sometimes I hate being a shade,' he said as his hand continued to pass through the handle as if it wasn't there.

Ezzy turned around to see what Slink was doing. Despite everything, she laughed manically. 'Slink, I love you just the way you are,' she said, 'please don't change.'

Working his way through the gears, the van began to pick up speed as Eli pressed the accelerator down as far as it would go. 'Which way, Ezzy?' he asked.

Ezzy frowned. 'Follow the road until we reach the crossing,' she said, suddenly thinking about where they were heading, 'then turn right.' She pulled her mobile out of her pocket and started at the empty signal indicator. There was no one to phone. No website that could help.

And Zam was going to meet her mum again.

Zam guided Q high into the sky and stared down at the ice cream van driving through the underworld streets of Newcastle with *The Magic Roundabout* theme echoing all around. The mannequins continued to chase after them but the gap between his friends and the screeching horde grew larger as the van began to pick up speed. Satisfied his friends were safe for now, Zam relaxed and the fact he was flying suddenly sank in. 'Q, you can fly,' he said, 'you're amazing.'

'Yeah I guess I am pretty cool, Kid,' Q said in an indifferent Han Solo voice, 'it's all part of the package of being a superhero.'

'A superhero?'

'Yeah, I know. I expect you think it's all about posing for pictures and signing autographs. It couldn't be further from the truth. Being a superhero I've got a whole load of other things keeping me occupied.'

'You do? Like what?'

'Oh you know, saving the world, saving up enough money for my retirement and finding the robot girl of my dreams.'

'Dreams, you have dreams, Q?'

'Of course I do, what else do you think happens when I sleep?'

'I'm not sure. I guess I thought you just went blank, like a TV does when you switch it off.'

'You think I'm like a TV?'

'No, what I meant is that when your power is switched off, I expected everything to be switched off. I guess you have a reserve power supply that keeps you, err, alive when your main power is switched off, right?'

'Correct, and it doesn't need food, water and air to keep it going like yours does.'

'What else do you dream about, Q?'

'Flying. I've always wanted to fly.'

'Me too. And now we are flying.'

'Yeah kid, we really are flying. Hey, it looks like dreams really do come true.'

'Not every dream comes true. I still can't walk.'

'Yeah, but flying must be better than walking, right? I know it's better than getting around on wheels.'

'I suppose it is, but even when I'm flying, I'm different to everyone else.'

'Being different is a good thing. It would be a dull world if all you guys looked like Brad Pitt.' Q's voiced changed from Han Solo to C-3P0. 'Or all robots looked like C-3P0. Do you think I look like C-3P0 by the way?'

Zam laughed, 'You're a wheelchair. How could you look like C-3P0?'

'In my dreams I look like C-3PO.'

'What does your girl look like in your dreams?'

'In my dreams she is a bomb disposal unit and her voice sounds like Lisa Simpson. I could listen to her speak all day long. She has such a kind, sorrowful voice. There is a lot of sadness inside my girl.'

'You are in love with a dream that looks like a bomb disposal robot and sounds like Homer's daughter from *The Simpsons*?'

'Yeah, I know. What a fantastic combination, huh?'

'It's... unusual.'

'Unusual?'

'Yeah, I mean, I don't really know what a robot would find attractive. I guess I thought you'd like someone who looked similar to you.'

'Would you like someone who looked the same as you?'

'I didn't mean it that way, I was thinking, you know – elephants are attracted to other elephants, dolphins to other dolphins, wheelchair robots to other wheelchair robots.'

'You don't like my girl do you?'

'I've never met her. And anyway, I do like her; she sounds like a lovely... girl.'

'She is lovely, I only hope I get to meet her one day.'

Zam looked down at the streets below where men, women, children and everything that should have been alive stood perfectly immobile, frozen in whatever pose they had been doing when time decided to stand still. While those things that should not have been alive – mannequins and statues and even paintings or pictures of humans that had stepped out of their frames – walked the streets as though it had never been any different.

And now, two gargoyles headed straight towards Zam, gargoyles he recognised from Christ Church. They flew towards him, grey and stone-like, with smiles fixed eternal that should never have been smiles, more statements of psychosis. Despite their stone form, they flew with the precision and dexterity of hummingbirds.

'See those buttons on top of the joysticks?' Q said, aware of the danger racing towards them.

Zam looked down at the joysticks, seeing the buttons for the first time. 'Yeah,' he said, placing his thumbs on top of them.

'Try pressing the right one.'

Zam pressed the button and a green laser sight suddenly appeared in front.

'Now press the left...'

Before Q had finished speaking, Zam pressed the left button and his animated smile looked exactly as it should on a fifteen year old boy discovering new possibilities as a red laser came from the left armrest and zapped the air in precisely the spot where the green laser sight ended.

Keeping the laser sight button pressed, Zam tried to guide Q until the sight touched the first gargoyle. It was too difficult positioning the sight though, as the wind buffeted him and his lack of flying experience meant he lurched from one position to the next. When the gargoyle looked like it was about to crash right into them, he pulled on the joysticks and veered off to the left just before contact occurred.

'This is going to be tricky, haven't you got a guided missile system or something else in your armrest that's a bit more high-tech?'

'Negative. This one is down to you, Napoleon,' Q said in Grandfather's voice.

Zam didn't have time to respond as the second kamikaze gargoyle attempted to do what the first had failed at and narrowly missed Zam as he pulled fully back on the joysticks and Q flew vertically into the air.

'Wooooo...' Zam yelled as his stomach felt like it had been left behind. He also felt something scamper down his side and realised that Rat had fallen out of his pocket. Quickly pushing the joysticks forward, Zam levelled Q off and desperately looked around, attempting to find Rat. Relieved, he saw that Rat had bitten into his jacket and locked his jaw like only a polecat can. Nothing can budge a polecat once its jaws are locked, except for choking it half to death, and Zam knew Rat would be safe from falling while he remained that way. What Zam didn't know was where the gargoyles were. He looked back and saw they were behind him and he swung Q around to face them. Without thinking about what he was doing he pressed the red laser button and kept it pressed, watching it arc across the sky until it hit one of the gargoyles.

As soon as the laser touched it, the gargoyle exploded into a million pieces. *Probably more than a million pieces,* Zam thought. 'Q, you're the best,' he yelled. 'Now let's go get ourselves another gargoyle.'

Feeling more confident than he had ever been in his entire life when the second gargoyle flew directly at him, this time Zam didn't veer away. This time he held the line and, half a second before impact, he pressed the button and closed his eyes as the air exploded in front of him and he flew through a dust cloud of gargoyle. 'Yeeees....' Zam yelled. 'Yes, yes, yes!'

Zam was still smiling when he remembered Ezzy and Grandfather. He stopped smiling and looked around, trying to get his bearings. They were above St James Park, but the football ground looked tiny down below and Zam realised how high up they had flown. He gazed up and the shifting red clouds looked far too close and full of dark secrets. Pushing forward on the joysticks, they glided downwards with only the low hum of Q's propulsion system and the breeze making any sound. As they descended further and flew above the streets of Newcastle once more, there were no other sounds and Zam suddenly realised how eerie it made his home town appear, even if it was his home town in the underworld.

Feeling Rat squirm, Zam left hold of the joysticks and Q kept them steady while he held his polecat in his hands and coaxed his jaw loose using gentle words and by stroking Rat's belly. 'I'm sorry I frightened you again,' he said to Rat when he finally released his teeth from Zam's jacket.

Rat nipped Zam's finger in response, then began to lick his hand.

'I guess I deserved that. Hang on, maybe I can make it up to you.' Zam pulled a paper bag from his jacket pocket and took a piece of cheese from it. 'There you go, boy. It's your favourite: Wensleydale.'

Rat greedily ate the cheese and when he finished he looked up at Zam, expecting more.

'Okay, boy,' Zam said. 'I guess just this once I can give you more than I should.'

When Rat finished eating the cheese, Zam put him back inside his pocket and this time fastened the zip so that Rat wouldn't fall out. Then he took hold of the joysticks and flew through the underworld, feeling like a superhero who had only just started to realise what he was really capable of doing.

14

Ezzy lived in Jesmond, a Victorian suburb ten minutes' walk from the city centre. Zam guided Q across Leazes Terrace heading towards Haymarket then followed The Great North Road before crossing the A167 into Jesmond. He saw the ice cream van parked in front of Ezzy's house in Fern Avenue. Scanning the area, Zam could only see one person in the street, a woman who was sweeping her hand through her hair with a big old smile on her face. She was in mid-step crossing the road and Zam thought how lucky she was, frozen in happiness for eternity. Relieved to see there were no mannequins or gargoyles or any other form of non-human creatures walking around, he guided Q over to the van and saw that Grandfather and Ezzy were not around. The front door to Ezzy's house was open and he guessed she would be inside.

'I think it's time you became a wheelchair again, Q,' Zam said, not sure if he wanted Ezzy's mother to be home or not.

Q started to morph back into the shape of a wheelchair in mid-air and when his wheels returned to their normal position and the propulsion system went silent, he dropped to the ground and Zam was sad that his maiden flight was over.

'I thought you said you couldn't fly?' Zam said as he wheeled himself into Ezzy's house.

'I couldn't fly when I was in Napoleon Mode,' Q replied. 'But when your grandfather set me to Combat Mode, the functions I could access changed and the ability to fly became available to me.'

'What other secrets haven't you told me about?'

'Only the ones I have to keep secret.'

'Funny, Q. Very funny. Are you sure you're not really Grandfather in disguise?'

'You guessed it, I really am Grandfather,' Q said, in a perfect grandfather voice. 'The one you left with Ezzy is really Q in disguise.'

Zam smiled as he wheelied Q into Ezzy's doorway with Q's motors helping to drive the rear wheels over the step. 'I wondered why he always smelled of engine oil. And now it makes perfect sense why you are always following me around like I can't look out for myself.'

'Can you keep a secret, Zam?'

'Yeah,' Zam said too quickly as he stopped pushing Q and waited for him to speak.

'Well, I'm not really your grandfather.'

'Ha. And I thought you were gonna tell me about the secret of life or something.'

'Do you think I'd still be rolling around like a wheelchair if I knew that secret?'

'I guess not.'

'No, I'd be... I'd be. I don't know, I think I'd be a horse.'

'A horse?'

'Yes, imagine what it would be like running wild on the open plain with nothing but the wind in your face and the sun on your back.'

'You mean, the wind in your face and a rider on your back? A bit like you are now with me in your seat.'

'I hadn't thought about that. I guess all I'd be doing is swapping four wheels for four legs.'

'Sorry, Q. I didn't mean to ruin your dreams.'

Q coughed and spoke in an English gentleman kind of way. 'Nonsense, I don't have any dreams, I'm a... a silicon chip. That's all. A series of circuits and electrical signals.'

'Just like I'm a series of electrical signals in a soft nervous tissue called a brain.'

'That's it, Zam, you've just revealed the secret of life.'

'I have?'

'Yes.'

'So what is it then?'

'Life is what you make of it.'

'I want to make my life the same as everyone else's. I want to be able to walk,' Zam said, grabbing hold of Q's wheels and pushing himself along the hallway. 'I think it's time we found out what the others are up to, and time you stopped acting like a dreamer.'

15

Zam entered the lounge and stared at Ezzy who was kneeling in front of her mother holding onto her hands. Mrs Ripley sat in the chair she always sat in, watching the TV she always watched. Only this time the television screen was blank, as dead as a fallen war hero. At first Zam thought Mrs Ripley wasn't frozen like the other people they had encountered in the underworld. It wasn't that she was moving; she remained fixed to her seat. Mrs Ripley always looked lifeless every time Zam saw her. Frozen in front of the television watching mindless daytime TV programs. Seeing her eyes remain fixed, unblinking, he knew then she was exactly like the others, a petrified copy of someone who didn't belong in the underworld. Studying her without any concern that she would turn around, wondering why he was staring at her, Zam suddenly saw Ezzy's face hiding in Mrs Ripley's, as if he was looking at a face within a face. Only Ezzy's features weren't filled with sorrow like her mother's and the skin around Ezzy's eyes wasn't lined with anguish, as if she spent her nights weeping alone. And Ezzy's eyes – where her eyes sparkled with curiosity and something more Zam wanted to believe was true; Mrs Ripley's eyes were blank, like a TV screen in the underworld.

Zam wondered how long it took someone to get over the death of a loved one. After six and a half years, Mrs Ripley still hadn't gotten over the death of her husband. She seemed worse each time Zam saw her. Yet Ezzy, although she was still affected by her father's death, looked better and better every time Zam saw her.

'Mum, can you hear me? Please talk to me,' Ezzy cried.

'Ezzy, this is not your mother,' Eli gently said. 'This is not your home. We are in the underworld and everything is a copy of everything you know. None of this is real.'

Zam looked around. As far as he could tell, the house looked the same as Ezzy's house. Yet there was something he couldn't quite place. His eyes glanced across at the star-shaped clock on the wall. The second hand was moving. It never moved. The clock had been broken for ages but for some reason Mrs Ripley didn't want to replace it. The clock started to tick inside his mind, but it wasn't quite the same sound as it should have been. As he continued to stare at the clock, he realised it was ticking the seconds away backwards. The sound it made grew louder inside his head and began to reverberate to his core. Like the clock's second hand, Zam started to go backwards too; backwards inside his mind, back towards those things he thought he'd buried forever. Jenson Murgo pushing his wheelchair through the park, even though Zam told him not to. Pushing him through the trees, too fast. His front wheel hitting the tree root and his wheelchair tipping over and Zam falling to the ground. Murgo leaving him there, running off laughing and shouting those words. Those hurtful words.

In the town centre next, every time he saw Murgo and his mate Richie Walsh. They squirted him with water pistols, or pulled his arms and legs. Flicked his ears and laughed.

Primary school next. How he hated his name. All those children in the playground calling him Nappy.

'Nappy, Nappy, Nappy. Soggy as a baby's nappy,' they chanted. Every child in the playground.

Everyone laughing.

He started to feel drowsy.

Tock, tick.

Louder.

Tock, tick.

Louder.

Tock, tick....

It was so easy to sleep. Everything bad would disappear if only he slept. All those things he wanted to forget from his past. All those things he was frightened about in the future. He wouldn't have to worry about getting a job he could be good at in a wheelchair. And it wouldn't matter if he never had a girlfriend. And children, he always thought he would never have his own children. Even though he wanted children. A son, a daughter. How could he be a father in a wheelchair? Now it didn't matter. Now he could sleep.

'That's right, Zam, sleep,' the voice ticked inside his head.

Then electricity.

Through his hands first, then sparking throughout his body.

He'd been electrocuted.

The clock stopped moving. It no longer made a sound.

'Zam,' he heard Q yelling in the voice of Johnny Depp.

Zam had always thought Johnny Depp would make a perfect father. He had sometimes wondered what it would be like to have a father like him. To be a father like him. Now he wondered why Q had used Johnny's voice to speak to him.

'You electrocuted me?' Zam said.

'I had to, you were drifting away,' Q replied, speaking in the voice of Captain Jack Sparrow.

'Now I'm tingling, tingling all over. Couldn't you have just shouted or something?' More than the tingling sensation, Zam tried to put the bad thoughts out of his mind. Those thoughts had no place in his real life or the weird life he had in the underworld.

Q prodded Zam with his robotic arm. 'I did shout, but you didn't respond. Neither did the others.'

Zam looked at Ezzy who was now standing in front of her mother.

'I've always been afraid of mannequins,' she said, 'since I was a young child. Nana had one in her back room. She was a dressmaker. She used to leave me alone with it when Mum went out to work. It kept staring at me; like it was my fault it didn't have any arms or legs.'

'Ezzy...' Zam said.

'No matter where I was in the room its eyes followed me, seeing everything.'

'You were only a child. I used to be frightened of clowns when I was younger, but not anymore.'

'Now I know it really was alive.'

'No, it wasn't. It's this place, messing with you. This isn't our world. This is someplace else. Someplace where we don't belong.'

'You're wrong, Zam; the place we came from isn't real. It never was; this is where we belong. I can feel it's real.'

Zam could see he was losing Ezzy. He could see it in her eyes. 'Help me,' he said, turning towards Grandfather. When he looked into his eyes, he saw the same blank expression.

'Q, what is it? What's happening to them?'

Q reverted to his favourite C-3P0 voice, 'I'm detecting a high frequency pulse, perfectly synchronous, like a clock ticking, but at the same time not like a clock ticking. Can't you hear it?'

'Not any more,' Zam said, wheeling towards Ezzy and

shaking her. Ezzy didn't respond; she simply stared ahead with empty eyes. 'Are you still in combat mode?' he asked Q.

'Affirmative. Until directed otherwise.'

'Okay, let me see those joysticks again.'

Q's joysticks whirred up from his armrests and Zam immediately grabbed hold of them, aiming for the clock on the wall. He zapped the clock and it shattered into pieces with a crashing sound that echoed around the room. When he looked at Ezzy and Grandfather they remained the same.

'Okay, so it wasn't the clock,' Zam said. 'Maybe we need something more substantial.' Wheeling Q around, he aimed at the bay window, thinking about bullies with water pistols who flicked people's ears. He pressed the fire button and continued to hold it down until the bay window and half the wall was blasted away. 'Damn, my ears are ringing!' Zam shouted as building dust plumed into the room.

'Can I ask what it is you are trying to do?' Q said.

'I'm trying to shake Ezzy and Grandfather out of the mind warp they are in.'

'Oh, I see. I thought maybe you just liked destroying things.'

Zam's grip tightened on the joysticks. 'Have you got a better idea?'

Q's motors began to whirr into life and the joysticks were pulled from Zam's grasp as they disappeared into the armrests.

'We could try electrotherapy. It worked on you after all.'

'You mean we should electrocute them?'

'Precisely.'

'How do we do that?'

'Like this,' Q said, as a charge of electricity shot from his armrest, hitting first Eli then Ezzy.

Shocked by the power of the electric charge coming from Q, Zam could only stare and hope Grandfather and Ezzy would recover from it as they violently twitched and shook in front of him. 'Do you really need to zap them with so much energy?'

Q stopped generating the charge. 'I'm not sure. Apart from when I zapped you, this is the first time I've done this sort of thing.'

Just as Zam started to think Ezzy would never stop shaking, she did stop and then she started to rub her temples.

'What...What happened?' she asked.

Zam smiled and touched Ezzy's arm. 'Q electrocuted you.'

Eli began to cough as he breathed in the dust still suspended in the air. 'What happened to the wall?'

'That would be Zam,' Q said.

'You sure equipped Q with some great gadgets,' Zam quickly spoke. 'You're the best, Grandfather.'

Eli frowned, 'Some gadgets are best kept from the hands of children.'

'He was superb fighting gargoyles,' Q said. 'And flying too. He's a natural.'

Ezzy looked down at her mum who was covered in dust but who also remained lifeless. She turned towards Q. 'Can you wake Mum the same way you woke me?'

'I'm afraid not,' Q said. 'This isn't your mother. This is a creature of the underworld.'

'Please try. Just in case you're wrong.'

'Yes, for Ezzy. Please try, Q,' Zam said.

Q sighed, exactly like a robot shouldn't sigh, but nevertheless, a stream of electricity shot from him and attached itself to Ezzy's mum for a few seconds. When the electric bolt subsided, Zam thought he saw Mrs Ripley's eyes sparkle for a second. And her mouth, it looked like it was about to open. Then every part of her began to move as she started to melt, like a Barbie doll in a microwave set at full power. She melted until she was no more than a plastic mound bubbling on the floor.

'I'm so sorry, Ezzy,' Q said.

Ezzy closed her eyes and began to cry. Eli quickly walked over to her side and put his arm around her.

'That wasn't your mother, Esmeralda,' he said, 'your mother is fine and well in Newcastle.'

'I hate this place,' Ezzy said.

Eli began to walk her out of the house. 'I know, Ezzy. I know.'

Zam followed close behind, wishing he could have been the one comforting Ezzy. Wishing he could have been the one walking by her side now.

16

'Where's Slink?' Zam asked.

Ezzy had stopped crying. She was standing with Grandfather, next to the ice cream van. They were talking too low for Zam to hear.

Eli turned towards Zam. 'He didn't want to come in the house. He said it didn't feel right. We left him outside to wait for you.'

Zam felt annoyed when Grandfather turned his back on him and started talking to Ezzy in that low voice again. Seeing Ezzy look more like her old self made him feel better though.

'Can you sense where Slink is?' he eventually asked Q.

'Negative,' Q replied. 'Sensing the presence of a ghost is beyond my capabilities. Why don't you call out for him?'

'I thought of doing that,' Zam said indignantly. 'I just wondered if you could sense him, that's all.'

'Oh, I see.'

'See what?'

Q cleared his throat. 'Err, nothing,' he said in Zam's voice.

Zam was about to question Q further, but thought better of it. 'Slink! Slink!' he shouted.

There was no reply.

'Maybe the explosion scared him off,' Q said.

Zam suddenly felt foolish. He knew that blasting the wall to pieces wouldn't have woken Grandfather or Ezzy from the trance they were in, but at the time, he needed to blast something to pieces. He leant back and stared at the clouds shifting impossibly fast in the red sky above and wondered if there was a sun behind them casting light or if there was some other means of illumination. Sitting upright, he scanned the area looking for shadows, trying to estimate the time of day. There were no shadows anywhere; it was as if there was more than one sun in the sky covering all angles so that shadows could never be cast in the underworld. As Zam continued to look around he noticed there was one shadow, though, next to the lamppost outside Ezzy's house. He smiled. 'I know where Slink is,' he said, grabbing Q's wheels and pushing them towards the lamppost.

'Are you okay, Slink?' Zam asked when he reached the lamppost.

There was no reply.

'I know you're here. Did the explosion frighten you?'

Still no reply.

'I'm sorry if it did. I... I needed to let off some steam. I've needed to do that for some time.' Zam waited a moment longer without speaking, giving Slink time to think on his words. When Slink still didn't respond, Zam spoke again. 'I'm okay now, though. I'm kinda realising it doesn't matter what people think about you. It doesn't matter if they laugh. Life is what you make it. Kinda.'

'It wasn't the explosion,' Slink said.

Zam looked down at Slink's shape on the ground. 'Your shadow makes a good lamppost.'

'How did you know it was me?'

'There aren't any shadows in the underworld.'

'Oh, I guess I'm unique then.'

'That's never been in doubt, Slink. Hey, tell me what frightened you?'

Slink's shadow wavered. 'It was the house. It didn't feel right. It felt like Mandrake Ackx.'

'Something in the house made us think bad things,' Zam said. 'It wanted us to sleep forever. Do you think it was Ackx?'

'I don't know. I just felt the house trying to pull me deeper into the underworld.'

'How much deeper can we go?'

'I think you have to die to go deeper. Maybe that's what the house was trying to do, take your life force away.' Slink stood up. 'I'm sorry for being a coward. I don't belong in your gang. I'm not a true Lion of the Wood.'

'You aren't a coward and our gang wouldn't be the same without you. You're a member for life.'

'But I'm dead already.'

'Then you're a member for eternity. In life and death, Lions of the Wood stand together forever.'

Slink's eyes suddenly appeared and Zam was sure he saw a smile cross his shadowy features.

'There's something I've been meaning to ask you, Zam.'

'Fire away. You can ask me anything.'

'Do you know why my arm is tied in a knot?'

Zam sighed. 'Let's go see what the others are doing,' he said, turning from Slink and wheeling himself over to Grandfather and Ezzy.

17

'I'm famished, and thirsty too,' Zam said to Grandfather. 'Are we okay eating underworld food?'

'If you can find any, yes, it should be safe.'

'We could try an ice cream,' Ezzy said. 'We have a whole van full of ice cream.'

Zam smiled at the thought of ice cream, but more so, he was pleased to see Ezzy look like her old self, not like her old mum. 'Ice cream is perfect.'

Ezzy didn't need any more encouragement. She left Eli's side and entered the ice cream van where she picked up a cone and filled it full of ice cream. 'Do you want a chocolate flake, Zam?'

'Nah, I want two flakes.'

Ezzy laughed and Zam thought the underworld wasn't so bad after all. She handed him the ice cream and he licked it hungrily and noisily.

'Damn, this is gorgeous,' he said. 'Underworld food kinda tastes the same but, I dunno, it's like it is the first time you try something new.'

Rat suddenly started to move around in Zam's pocket and as Zam unzipped it, Rat's head popped out and he sniffed the air expectantly.

'Here you go boy,' Zam said, taking one of the chocolate flakes from his ice cream and offering it to his polecat. Rat gently took the flake in his teeth and curled up on Zam's lap, licking the flake and biting small pieces off before eating it with his eyes closed. He always closed his eyes when he ate and Zam wondered what was going through his head while he was eating that way.

Zam closed his eyes and licked the ice cream.

'I think I get it now, Rat. Things taste different in the dark, it's like you aren't distracted from the taste and you get to appreciate the full flavour.' He opened his eyes and saw Rat sitting up, staring at him. 'I guess you are wondering what's going through my head, right?'

Rat sniffed the air and seemed to nod his head at the same time, as if he was agreeing with Zam.

Ezzy quickly pulled two more ice creams, handing one to Eli and keeping the other for herself and the three of them stood beneath the underworld's shifting red sky, eating hungrily and talking nonsense.

'I miss food more than anything else I can remember,' Slink said after they had finished eating.

'I'm sorry, Slink,' Ezzy said. 'I didn't think...'

'It's okay. I enjoyed watching you all eating.'

'It's me who should be sorry, Benjamin,' Eli said. 'If

only I hadn't been so full of myself thinking I could make something that could talk to Time.'

'Grandfather, you're beginning to sound as bad as me moaning. Everything is Ackx's fault.' Zam wheeled around in a circle, staring at them. 'Don't any of you forget that.'

They never heard Ackx approach. Never knew he was there until he first spoke. 'Brave words from one so young. One so – unsteady on his feet.'

Zam spun around and saw Ackx standing by the lamppost. He was the same creature he had seen in the cavern, but he no longer resembled a mangled bag of bones. He now stood over seven feet tall on slender legs bent at the knees as if he was about to spring forward. His face was gaunt with angular cheekbones that stuck out because the rest of his face had wasted away, while his nose was bent and misshapen, bearing the scars of a battle fought sometime in the distant past. He wore an expensive suit, the type of garment that shouldn't have been worn by a creature such as Ackx and it made him appear ludicrous but at the same time profoundly menacing. Ackx's voice affected Zam more so than his appearance. It made his spine feel like it was trying to crawl out of his body. Shrill, yet measured, it sounded like a voice you only heard in a bad dream. One you could never quite describe. A voice that always filled you with dread whenever it came to mind.

The changeling sat by Ackx's side with a disinterested

122

look on its face. Rat stared at the changeling and raised his hackles, hissing a warning. The changeling yawned, then morphed into a black polecat the size of a lion and hissed at Rat with an intensity that frightened Zam like no other sound had before. It resonated inside him, like the prickly sensation of having to stand outside a darkened room full of your most terrifying nightmares, knowing the door would slowly close behind you once you stepped inside.

Rat sat back down on Zam's lap and began to lick his paws like he was the coolest polecat on the block. The changeling turned towards Ackx, looking for direction.

Ackx ignored the changeling and stared intently at Ezzy. The way Ackx watched her, like he was staring at something he shouldn't be staring at, strengthened Zam's resolve. 'What do you want?' he asked, not sure what else to say. Pleased to hear his voice steady and unwavering.

Ackx didn't reply; instead, he bent his long neck forward and walked towards Zam, leaning on his cane for support. As he approached, Zam couldn't help but stare at the awkward way the wyte moved. It was as if he was a child learning to walk for the first time. The way he jerked and rocked as each leg took it in turns to reach out to the ground in front of the other made Zam feel deathly uncomfortable. Was this what others saw whenever he tried to move without the aid of his leg splints or his walking frame?

Zam flinched when Ackx eventually reached him, but

Ackx didn't stop; he walked past Zam like he didn't exist and stopped next to Ezzy.

'I am sorry for your loss, child,' he said when he reached her. His hand moved to touch her face, but at the last moment it remained frozen in the air with its long bony fingers spread wide and needy.

'My loss?' Ezzy said, backing away from Ackx's touch.

Ackx's eyes blinked rapidly. 'Yes, your father. I feel the same intense emotion you feel. It is the same for everyone who loses a parent when so young.' His eyes remained open when he finished speaking. Black pools of awareness glistening intense longing.

Ezzy didn't want to look into his eyes and she glanced from side to side, seeking an excuse not to look. Seeing Eli, seeing Zam, only made her feel worse when she saw nothing but concern on both their faces. 'How do you know what it's like to lose your father?' she said, and despite everything she couldn't help being drawn to those eyes.

Ackx smiled without showing his teeth. 'When I was a child I also lost my father.' As he talked, he started to grow smaller until he stood only a few inches taller than Ezzy and he no longer appeared bent or misshapen. As if his previous disabled appearance had been a trick of the underworld light. 'The loss of a father has a profound effect on a child,' he continued, 'no matter how cruel the father is to the child.'

The more Ezzy looked into his eyes, the more they

reminded her of her father's eyes. And when he raised his hand to gently touch her cheek, she did not flinch away. 'My father wasn't cruel,' she whispered.

Ezzy never saw Ackx's lips move, but she heard his gentle, understanding voice inside her head. 'Don't blame yourself, dear child. Never forget, the responsibility does not lie with you.'

A single teardrop began to fall from Ezzy's eye.

'Leave the child alone, Mandrake,' Eli carefully but firmly said. 'It's me you need. Let her and Napoleon go and I'll start working on the Relater again.'

Ackx stopped the teardrop falling any further down Ezzy's cheek with his thumb and retraced its path until he reached her eye. He paused for a moment before wiping the remaining tear away. Without hesitating, he then wiped his thumb across his lips.

'Mandrake!' Eli yelled.

Ackx continued to stare at Ezzy while he spoke. 'Your time is over, old friend. I no longer trust you and when trust lies abandoned in the dirt so too does everything else.' His hand moved towards Ezzy's hair and as his fingers entwined themselves in her strands, his eyes seemed to sparkle even more.

'Get your hands off her!' Zam yelled, wheeling himself towards Ackx.

The changeling had been watching Zam and, like an obedient foot soldier protecting its master, it leapt at Zam when he threatened Ackx. All the while, Rat had fixed his gaze on the changeling and before it reached Zam, Rat shot towards the changeling, landing on its snout before it reached Zam. Rat scratched at the beast's eyes and bared his teeth, hissing a warning of intent. The changeling raged as it reared up on its hind legs, attempting to rip Rat from its snout with its front paws. Rat sunk his teeth into the changeling's ear and locked his jaws and the changeling growled in rage, as it attempted to loosen Rat from its ear.

'Rat, no!' Zam yelled as he saw his tiny friend look even tinier against the changeling's black mass.

The changeling's paws began to morph into claw-like hands, as its grip on Rat tightened and it squeezed the life out of the polecat. With a desperate gasp, Rat eventually released his jaws and the changeling's maw engulfed him as it shook its head from side to side with Rat's rear legs sticking out of its mouth. Shaking its head one last time, the changeling opened its jaws and Zam watched helplessly as his friend flew through the air and landed on the hard surface of the road where he remained, unmoving.

Staring through tears, Zam aimed the sight at the changeling and pressed the laser button, hitting the beast directly in the chest. Yellow blood exploded from the changeling as it was knocked backwards by the force of the laser. Without waiting to see if the changeling was dead, Zam rushed over to Rat and gently picked him up from the road. His friend was no more than a clump of crushed bone and slaver-wet fur. Zam closed his eyes and hugged Rat into his chest. 'I'm sorry, Rat. I'm so sorry...'

Hearing Zam's words, Ezzy wrenched her eyes from Ackx. 'Zam...' she started to say, making a move towards him.

'I have never had a daughter as beautiful as you,' Ackx said, running his fingers through Ezzy's hair, stopping her from going to Zam.

Zam's eyes shot open at the sound of Ackx's voice and he gently placed Rat's crushed body into his pocket before zipping it up. Wheeling around, ready to blast the changeling's head off before he dealt with Ackx, he froze. The changeling no longer resembled the beast that killed his friend. Now it was a small child, a girl no more than five years old.

'Yes,' Ackx said without taking his eyes off Ezzy. 'She is only a child. Finish her off if it pleases you.'

Zam's fists clenched the joysticks but he did not fire the laser. Instead, he twisted around and faced Ackx. 'Turn around, wyte,' he managed to gasp while holding back tears.

Ackx continued to stare at Ezzy as he talked to Zam. 'She heals quickly. If you do not finish what you started, the consequences will be severe.'

'I said turn around, wyte.'

Eli stepped in between Zam and Ackx. 'Napoleon, you can't do this.'

Zam's mouth gaped open. He couldn't believe what Grandfather was doing. 'Rat is dead.'

'I know, but you still must not do this.'

Zam could feel himself shaking and he stared at the ground, not wanting to see the look on his grandfather's face as he pulled free from him. 'Ezzy, move away from that freak,' he managed to say, unable to believe he had used that word. He hated the freak word. Hated being called it so many times in the past.

Somewhere in her mind Ezzy heard Zam speak and she wanted to do as he said, but looking into Mandrake's eyes she wanted to stay with him more. His now blue eyes were just like her father's, gentle and kind and full of humour. And Mandrake's hair, now dark and wavy, it too was just like her father's. If she let herself believe, just a little, Mandrake could almost be her father.

'Ezzy,' Zam yelled. 'Look at me. Don't let him get inside your head.' Pushing hard on the joysticks, Q suddenly shot forwards, bundling Eli aside. When he reached Ackx, Zam kicked out at him. 'Leave her alone,' he yelled.

Ackx stumbled forwards into Ezzy and his arms encircled her as he regained his balance.

'Zam, what are you doing?' Ezzy screamed, as Ackx's demeanour began to change.

Seeing Ezzy defend Ackx made Zam angrier. 'What are you doing? Can't you see this thing is evil?'

Ackx stood at his full height once more and Ezzy gasped when she saw his face and his black eyes holding nothing but rage.

'Never touch me again,' Ackx said as he turned around and stared at Zam with his lips curled up and his teeth bared. 'Unless it is I who first touches you.'

Ackx bent into Zam, so quickly it was as if he had done it moments earlier, without Zam noticing. Before there was time to react, Ackx placed his hand on top of Zam's hand. As soon as he touched him, Zam could not move, or breathe, or scream. And how he wanted to scream. How he wanted to scream like he had never screamed before, as each and every cell in his body, every fragment of his being began to freeze in perfectly synchronised agonising pain.

'No!' Eli screamed as he dashed towards Ackx and went to push him away from Zam. Thankfully, just before he was about to touch Ackx, he managed to keep his emotions in check and held back. 'Mandrake, stop. The Relater works. It has always worked.'

Ackx's dead eyes widened. 'If you are lying, Eli...'

'You know I am not lying. Now please release your grip on my grandson or Time will never hear you speak.'

Ackx slowly did as Eli asked and Zam immediately began to shake and writhe, unable to control any part of his body.

Ezzy ran over to Zam. 'I'm sorry,' she said, taking hold of his arms, trying to get him to stop shaking. 'He's so cold,' she wept, looking at Eli.

'You and I and the girl need to return,' Ackx said, as he slowly morphed into a smaller form.

Eli bent down towards Zam, gently touching his forehead with the back of his hand. 'And Napoleon?'

'He can stay here.'

'He can't survive in the underworld alone,' Eli said, standing and facing Ackx.

'He has a shade. It can lead him back to his own world.'

'Ezzy must go with him, she doesn't belong here.'

Ackx leant on his cane and his posture became aged and crooked once more, as if the incredible speed and agility he had shown moments ago were merely an illusion. 'She belongs to me, Eli. It has always been this way since first she stepped into my world.'

'Mandrake, she…'

'The boy lives, does he not?'

Eli lowered his gaze.

'The weapon you made for the boy, I cannot allow it to remain.' Ackx turned towards Zam and, reaching down, he touched Q's armrest with a single bony finger.

At first, nothing happened. Then ice began to spider web across Q's framework and his metal components started to creak and groan as vapour rose from him.

'Zam,' Q said in an unfamiliar voice. 'Everything is turning black.'

'He won't be able to get out of the underworld without his wheelchair,' Eli pleaded.

Ackx ignored Eli as one of Q's wheels suddenly cracked in half and the wheelchair lurched to the side.

When the axle hit the ground the rest of the wheelchair shattered into innumerable pieces.

Ezzy tried to support Zam, but he fell to the ground, convulsing uncontrollably.

Ackx placed his hand on Ezzy's shoulder, smiling needle-sharp teeth. 'Do not be concerned, he can crawl out of the underworld.'

Ezzy wanted to pull away from Ackx. She wanted to tell him to keep his creepy hands off her. Wanted to harm Ackx like he had harmed Zam. Most of all, she desperately wanted to stay with Zam, to make sure he was going to live. He looked far from likely to do that and his eyes, they pleaded with her to stay with him more so than if he could shout it out aloud.

'And you my dear,' Ackx continued, 'you are going to behave exactly like a father expects a daughter to behave. Isn't that right?'

Ezzy could feel more than the weight of Ackx's hand on her shoulder as he spoke. There was a controlled energy emanating from his touch, like an electrical bolt frozen in ice that could suddenly spark into chaotic life if reason presented itself. And Ezzy didn't want to give Ackx a reason to unleash his power again. The look she saw in his eyes when he turned on Zam frightened her more than anything else in her life. More than that morning when they first heard the news about her father. The morning when her mother might as well have died too.

Staring into his eyes felt like gazing into supernatural insanity.

She stood up and Zam's eyes changed as she took Ackx's hand in her own. She would never forget how broken he looked when she did that. And turning her back on Zam she allowed Ackx to walk her into his terrifying world, feeling another kind of fear. The fear of losing more than a best friend.

At first, Zam could only move his fingers. Then he could stretch his hands and next his arms. When he could lift himself up he couldn't feel his toes, so he wiggled them back into life before eventually his feet and legs also responded to his instructions.

The changeling sat beside him all the while, watching without speaking as Zam's body returned to normality. It had kept the same childlike body of the young girl, but the hole Zam had blasted into its chest appeared to be fully healed. It wore no clothes, but its long black hair reached down to its legs concealing much of its perfectly white skin.

'Your friend was brave,' the changeling finally said, when Zam lifted himself up into a sitting position.

Zam hadn't wanted to think about Rat, not ever. Not have to think about how mangled he had become. 'You killed him.'

'He was trying to rip my ear off,' the changeling said in a voice too innocent and too childlike.

Zam wished the changeling would revert to looking

and sounding like a beast. It was difficult hating something that sounded and looked like a young girl. 'Why haven't you killed me already?'

The changeling yawned without covering its mouth. 'I have no reason to kill you.'

'You were going to attack me before. Before Rat stopped you.'

'You were going to attack my master. He is no longer my master.' The changeling started to wiggle its toes, similar to how Zam had moments before.

Zam frowned. 'Why are you still here?'

'I don't think she has anywhere else to go,' Slink said, as he stepped out of the ice cream van.

'It isn't a she. It's an it. A wild beast.' Zam rubbed his temples, his head pounded. Staring at Slink, Zam thought his friend looked different, smaller. Maybe it was the effects of what Ackx had done to him.

'You need something to drink,' Slink said. 'There's bottled water in the van, but I can't get it for you.'

The changeling stood up and walked over to the van. It came out a moment later with a bottle of water and offered it to Zam.

Zam looked up at the changeling and seeing the bottle of water he felt angry. He snatched the bottle from the changeling anyway and started to untwist the top.

'What's your name?' Slink asked the changeling.

'I already told you it's called "It",' Zam grunted as he started to drink the water.

The changeling moved away from Zam and began to skip around in circles on the pavement. 'My mother named me Hestia.'

'Nice name, ' Slink said, 'I'm called... ' he looked at Zam, 'what am I called again? Oh, and what are you called?'

'The old man called him Napoleon,' Hestia said.

Zam finished gulping down the water. 'I'm not called that, I'm called Zam.'

'Oh, right, Zam,' Slink said, gliding back and forth as he watched Hestia skipping. 'Cool name. What am I called then?'

'Slink.'

'Slink... Slink. I like Slink. It sounds cool. Cooler than Zam at least.'

'You look like a Slink,' Hestia said.

Slink glided over towards Hestia and began to follow her in circles, skipping as well a shade could skip. 'You mean I look cool?' he asked.

'No,' Hestia replied.

'What then?'

'It's an evasive thing. You look evasive.'

'Evasive in a cool kind of way?'

'I'm not sure what you mean. Do you mean you look cold?'

Slink laughed. 'Of course not, Hestia.'

'What do you mean then?'

Slink stopped skipping and when Hestia reached him,

she continued to skip and passed straight through him. 'I don't know either,' Slink said. 'I've forgotten what I was talking about.'

They both began to laugh, like children in a playground as Hestia continued to skip and continued to pass through Slink each time she reached him.

Zam tried to put their laughter out of his mind. Tried to recall everything that had happened since Rat had died. He remembered the incredible pain he felt when Ackx touched him, like he was freezing from the inside out. How could anything cause so much pain? And then he remembered Q. He looked down at the fragments he sat upon. Fragments of Q. His head pounded with renewed vigour as he shuffled away from what remained of his friend.

'Are you okay?' Slink asked in an unfamiliar childlike voice.

'Of course I'm not okay. Rat is dead and Q is gone.'

Slink clapped his hands behind his back, then in front of his chest, then behind his back again. 'Hey, don't forget about me. I'm dead too, remember?'

Zam dropped the bottle of water on the floor suddenly feeling drained and despite how hard he tried, he just couldn't stop himself as he lay down with his head in his arms and silently cried himself to sleep.

19

'Where has Ackx taken Grandfather and Ezzy?' Zam asked later when he awakened. His headache had subsided but the other ache remained.

Slink was playing hopscotch where a child had chalked a grid on the pavement. 'Grandfather and Ezzy?' he said. 'Who are Grandfather and Ezzy?'

Zam sighed and looked around for the changeling. He couldn't see her anywhere.

'Mandrake has taken them back to his hollow,' Hestia said.

Zam looked up at where the voice came from and saw Hestia sitting on top of the ice cream van, staring down at Slink. 'How do we get there?'

Hestia angled her head and began to stroke her hair with both her hands. 'You do not get anywhere. You cannot walk.'

Zam slid across to the ice cream van and pulled himself up. Using the side of the van for balance, he moved forward a few faltering steps. When he got to the end of the van, he made a move to step away from it, but nearly lost his balance and thought better of it. 'You're a changeling; change yourself into a wheelchair so I can ride you.'

'I cannot do that; I can only change into living creatures.'

'So change into a horse. No, not a horse. ' *Q wanted to be a horse, Zam suddenly remembered. He didn't want to be reminded of that conversation.* 'Change into a tiger. An alabaster tiger. I've always wanted to ride on an alabaster tiger.'

'No.'

'Why not?'

'No one has ever ridden on my back. No one rides a changeling.'

'You killed my friend. I could have killed you.' Zam's hand instinctively moved towards his pockets, searching for Rat. Rat was not there, but there was something else in his pocket.

'I could have killed you too,' Hestia said.

Zam pulled out a small electronic device from his pocket. It was the size and shape of a matchbox. He recognised it as something his grandfather carried around. 'But you didn't.'

'No.'

'Are you afraid of Ackx? Is that why you won't help me?'

'Yes, I am afraid of him, but that is not why I won't

help you.' Hestia watched Zam looking at the device. 'The old man put that in your pocket before he left.'

Zam didn't know what the device was used for. He put it back into his pocket and fastened the zip, wondering if Grandfather had removed Rat's body. 'If you take me to Ackx, I'll kill him. Then you won't have to fear him again.'

'Have you ever killed anyone before?'

Zam bit on his lip. 'No, but I've zapped a gargoyle and smashed a mannequin to pieces.'

'Why do you want to kill him?'

'He killed Q.'

'The wheelchair was never alive.'

'Q was my friend.'

'So was the polecat.'

'Yes.'

'Do you want to kill me?' Hestia asked.

'Yes. No. I mean, I did, but not anymore.'

'Why not anymore?'

Zam thought a while before answering. 'I don't know. Maybe I'll want to kill you again later. Anyway, Ackx is to blame for Rat. Everything is his fault.'

The ice cream van suddenly began to creak and rock from side to side as Hestia changed, becoming much larger than the small girl she was previously. When the transformation was complete, she jumped down from the van, landing next to Zam.

Zam was five feet, five inches tall, but the black tiger stood eye to eye with him and, staring into its unblinking eyes, he was sure the changeling was much older than a human could ever possibly be. Controlling the fear he felt rising inside his stomach, Zam managed to keep his voice steady when he spoke. 'I said an alabaster tiger, not a black tiger.'

'I do not do white. I only do black.'

'What's wrong with white?'

'There is nothing wrong with white. It's simply about who you are. You are either black or white.'

'Is this an underworld thing?'

'No, it is a Hestia thing. Tell me, are you black or white?'

'I've never thought about it before. I'm probably grey.'

'That makes you white.'

'No.'

'Black then, the same as me.'

'This is dumb. You're a changeling, you can do anything you want. That is, if you really want to.'

Hestia's eyes narrowed and two large canine teeth started to grow from her top jaw. 'What about these instead?' she said when the teeth stopped growing.

'Very nice,' Zam said, impatient now, 'but if I'd wanted a sabre-toothed tiger I would have asked for a sabre-toothed tiger.'

Hestia stared at Zam for a moment. 'Do not tell anyone,' she said, blinking once. Then she yawned into his face. Then her fur began to change colour until it was black and white striped.

'Where is Rat?' Zam asked, pleased that Hestia had done as he requested, but determined not to show it.

Hestia looked over her right shoulder, then to her left, clearly unhappy with her new look. She raised her head, sniffing the air. 'Your polecat was a warrior. He deserved a warrior's burial.'

'You buried him here in the underworld?'

'Yes.'

Zam pushed himself away from the ice cream van and stood as steady and as straight as he could. 'You should kneel down before me so I can get on your back.'

Hestia bared her teeth and Zam thought he had pushed the changeling too far, but she eventually did as Zam said anyway and before she could change her mind and eat him, Zam climbed on top of her. Unbalanced, he almost fell off her when she stood up.

'This feels undignified,' Hestia said.

Zam grabbed hold of her fur. 'Show me where you buried Rat.'

Hestia looked over her shoulder at Zam as if she was going to pull him off her back. Instead, she turned around and began to slowly walk over to Ezzy's house and into her front garden. She stopped by a wisteria growing against the garden wall.

Zam looked down and saw a fresh mound of earth beneath the vine. 'You call this a warrior's burial?'

'It is the sentiments at the time of the burial that make it so.'

'What sentiments?'

'My sentiments.'

'And what were your sentiments?'

'Sadness, regret, joy.'

'Joy?'

'Yes, joy. For one who sacrificed himself for another. Not every warrior is fortunate enough to die that way.'

Hestia's words made Zam feel worse. He gripped her neck fur tightly, ready to move on. 'Let's go find Ackx,' he said.

Hestia turned away from the garden and headed for Newcastle city centre. When she reached the ice cream van Slink jumped from the top of it, and landed behind Zam, placing his hands on top of his shoulders.

'Can we go to the Metro Centre? There's a rollercoaster there.' Slink said.

'No Slink, we haven't got time for a rollercoaster,' Zam said.

'There is always time for rollercoasters, Zam. How old are you anyway?'

'Old enough to know there are more important things than rollercoasters. How old are you anyway? You're acting even stranger than usual.'

'If you take me to the Metro Centre I promise not to act strange.'

'And how are you going to keep that promise?'

'Look at the sky, Zam. It's incredibly red and moving as fast as an express train.'

Zam gazed upwards. 'Is this the first time you've noticed the underworld sky?'

'I remember, remember the fifth of November. But I don't know why.'

'Slink you're starting to worry me.'

'Do you hear the voices? I never noticed them before.'

'What voices, Slink?'

'Every voice. Every voice that ever spoke.'

Zam turned around to look at Slink. 'You're not making any sense.'

'That's because there are too many voices. Too many to make sense.'

'I can't hear any voices, Slink.'

'Because you're not listening.'

'I can hear your voice. And… Hestia's voice.'

Slink shushed Zam. 'I can hear my mother's voice. She is talking to father about me. I haven't been born yet and already they are proud of me. I never thought they cared. It's the past. I can hear the past. And the future, Zam. Ackx is going to kill you later today. I heard him kill you. You mustn't go to him.'

'Slink stop; you're acting delusional.'

'Yes, delusional. Maybe that's why I can hear Rat speaking too. He has a Geordie accent. Can you believe that, a polecat with a Geordie accent? He is mocking you. In the future. Maybe you won't find Ackx after all and he won't kill you.'

'Or maybe I do find him and I put an end to him.'

'Are there any rollercoasters in Newcastle, Zam?'

'You know there are, Slink.'

'I do?'

'Yes, and if we ever get out of the underworld I'll take you to ride them.'

'You will? Promise?'

'Yeah, I promise Slink. One day I will take you for a ride on a rollercoaster at the Metro Centre.'

Slink jumped from Hestia's back and raced off in front of them.

'Where are you going?' Zam yelled after him.

Slink continued to race ahead and eventually disappeared from view. 'I don't think it's ever going to happen, Zam.' Slink's voice sounded all around. 'I've tried and I've tried but I can't hear any voices talking about me and you riding rollercoasters in the future.'

Zam sat up straight on top of Hestia, searching for Slink. It wasn't until a while later, when they turned into the high street, that he saw him. He was sitting by the side of the road next to an upturned bin with his head in his hands.

'I think you are going to die, Zam,' Slink said when they reached him. 'I think you are going to die.'

Zam stared down at Slink for a moment before speaking. 'If I do, then I'll be a ghost like you, Slink and I promise we will ride rollercoasters together from the moment the afterlife sun rises, until the moment it sets.'

Slink quickly stood up and Zam noticed that his

features were becoming more distinctive and less like a shadow.

'Then let's find Ackx as quickly as possible,' he said, climbing onto Hestia behind Zam. When he was settled he leaned into Zam and whispered into his ear. 'Because I want you to die now, Zam. I want you to die.'

20

I want you to die.

Sometimes, Zam wanted the same thing. Sometimes he just wanted to be able to walk like everyone else walked. Right now, he didn't want any more of his friends to die. Right now, he felt more alive than he had ever felt before. Maybe it was because Rat and Q were dead. He wondered why being so close to death made him feel so alive. He wondered if he would feel the same once he died too. A shiver leisurely inched its way down the length of his spine and he had the distinct feeling he was going to find out soon.

The journey through underworld's Newcastle had been easy, once Zam figured out that to keep his balance on top of an alabaster tiger he had to move his body in unison to the beast's gait. Better still, there were no psychotic mannequins roaming the streets. Hestia said it was because Ezzy wasn't travelling with them. The mannequins were her nightmare, no one else's. Ackx used her memories to manipulate the underworld, twisting it into an extension of Ezzy's fears.

Listening to Hestia's words, it felt like Zam had learned more about Ezzy in the short time they had been together in the underworld than all the time he had known her through school. It made him wonder what else he didn't know about Ezzy. Grandfather too, what other secrets had he kept from Zam?

What did he really know about anyone other than himself?

Zam decided to stop thinking about secrets and focused his attention on the deserted city instead. The silence of Newcastle city centre with only the sound of Hestia's paws padding against the footpath was incredibly relaxing. As long as he didn't think about Rat or Q. Even Slink seemed to fall easily into Zam's mood, hardly speaking a word throughout the journey. Despite the movement of the clouds above, the air in the underworld remained as still as if they were inside a sealed room. There was no breeze or shift in temperature from the moment he had stepped into this strange place, to him now sitting on the back of an alabaster tiger with sabre teeth. *Maybe I'm not really in the underworld*, he suddenly thought. *Maybe I'm under some kind of spell. A trick of the mind. A Mandrake Ackx trick.* Zam knew Ackx was messing with Ezzy's head. Why else would she look at someone as ugly as him like he was the saviour of the world or something, unless he was playing with her mind? And Grandfather, the only reason he left Zam lying there was because he thought the alternative meant Zam would be harmed further. He hoped he was right about both of them. He was sure he was right about both of them. Yet seeing Ezzy walk away with Ackx like Zam never existed, and Grandfather – *he never even looked back* – he couldn't help but wonder.

'Are you sure you want to do this?' Hestia asked. They had reached the railway station and she stopped at the arched entranceway.

'I have no other choice,' Zam replied, 'I can't leave Grandfather and Ezzy with Ackx.'

'Sometimes I think we never have a choice,' Hestia said, as she raised her leg and began to lick her paw. 'We simply follow a path that twists and turns but does not have any crossroads.'

'What would be the point of living a life like that?'

'To ensure we all reach the same ending.'

'If that's true, the ending is going to be extremely crowded.'

'Not if the ending is infinite.'

'Are you messing with my head?'

Hestia laughed, the first time Zam had heard her laugh. It was more than a laugh though, more like someone singing. It made Zam's spine tingle and he didn't want to feel that way about anything Hestia did. He stiffened up trying to stop the sensation in his spine and Hestia stopped laughing.

Zam suddenly felt empty.

'You can't defeat a wyte,' Hestia said, in the same voice she had spoken in when she was a young girl.

'I can try.'

'Yes, you can at least try.'

'Why did you work for Ackx?'

'I had no choice.'

'Here we go again.'

'He wanted me so I was his, like you have no choice but to breathe air.'

'I think you are taking this not having a choice thing too far.'

'Have you ever tried not breathing?'

Zam hadn't tried not breathing before. Just to prove a point, he stopped breathing, but it didn't last long. 'I still think you're wrong,' he finally gasped.

'Ackx is down there,' Hestia said, nodding her head towards a door at the end of some oil-stained steps descending into the ground. 'You will have to make your own way from here.'

Hestia smelled the same as Rat, Zam suddenly thought as he gulped in air mingled with her scent. She… Zam still didn't like to think of her as a she; the changeling wasn't bad smelling like Rat when he hadn't been cleaned for a while or when he was frightened, she had that wet fur smell Zam liked and he hated liking anything about Hestia. Even now, after all her help getting him around the underworld, he didn't like her. He appreciated what she had done for him as much as he could, but in the end she had killed Rat and he had to do something about that. To do nothing would be to betray Rat. He didn't know what to do yet, he just knew he had to do something. Yet he still liked that wet fur smell, the one that reminded him of Rat when Grandfather first brought his polecat home. It had rained that day and Rat's scent seemed to fill the whole apartment. It was so different to the old-age Grandfather smell he was used to and it made Zam feel different, like there was more to life than not being able to walk and school and bullies. The day Grandfather brought Rat home, Zam wasn't alone for what felt like the first time in his life. Now for the first time in a long time, Zam began to feel alone again.

And it wasn't even raining.

He thought about Ezzy and then tried his hardest not to think about her. 'I can't do this on my own, Hestia,' he said.

'I know.'

'Will you take me to Ackx?'

Hestia had told him there was an entrance to Ackx's cavern at the end of a disused maintenance shaft underneath the station's main platform. The maintenance shaft was behind the door she had just shown him. Zam didn't want to have to crawl the rest of the way on his hands and knees to reach Ackx, though he would if he had to.

'I don't want to,' Hestia said. 'Yet it suddenly feels like I don't have a choice.'

'I think this is one of those times when you do have a choice.'

Slink slid off Hestia and flicker walked over to her head. 'Stay with us, Hestia,' he said, scratching her ear without scratching it with his shade hand. 'You can join our gang and become a Lion of the Wood. On second thoughts, you can be an Alabaster Tiger of the Wood.'

Looking down at Slink, Zam was shocked to see how further Slink had changed. He now had the appearance of a teenage boy. A teenage boy who had the same translucent form as Yelena.

'Slink, are you okay?

'I've never felt better,' he laughed, running over to the taxis parked in front of the station. 'Now you see me, now you don't,' he yelled as he dissolved in and out of the taxis.

'Your shade will leave soon,' Hestia said.

'What do you mean?'

'Only the very strong or the very old can deny the light. He has never been strong, but he was very old after the Relater had finished aging him. He has been growing younger ever since. Rapidly so once he entered the underworld. When his awareness finally returns, so too will the light.'

Zam didn't want to lose another friend, but he had a feeling this was the best way to lose one if it had to happen. 'There was a girl in the tunnels under Newcastle. A ghost. She was looking for her mum. She wasn't old and she didn't look very strong.'

'The strength I talk of is defined by something much more subtle than appearance.'

'Like what?'

'In my language it is called Zigg. In your language it is known as determination, sentience, will, awareness and much more.'

'When you change into that girl, is that your true self?'

'I am changeling. I do not have a true self. Not while I live.'

Zam was reminded of Q when he said he didn't have a voice of his own. When his friend spoke those last few words, before he was gone, Zam hoped the voice he spoke in then was his own. 'What happens when you die?'

'I will follow the light.'

'What is this light you keep talking about?'

'You know what it is.'

'I don't believe in God.'

'You believe in shades and changelings and wytes though?'

Zam changed the subject, not wanting to continue where Hestia was leading him. 'Ackx said you were younger than you look. How old are you?'

'I am older than you.'

'I can tell you are very old, you never answer questions properly,' Zam absently started to stroke Hestia's neck. 'Okay, I only have one more question for you. Have you ever killed anyone?'

'Yes.'

'And you expect to go to heaven?'

'I expect to go wherever the light takes me.'

'I think you would have killed me and Grandfather and Ezzy if Ackx had asked you to.'

'If I was a Lion of the Wood and you asked me to kill a wyte, would I be any different?'

'Yes, because I would only ask you to do that if he was going to harm one of us.'

Slink ran up to them whistling *Twinkle Twinkle Little Star*. 'Anyone fancy a game of footy?'

'You haven't got any feet, Slink,' Zam said.

Slink looked down at his feet that weren't there. 'Wow, I wonder when I lost them. Do you think they'll grow back?'

'I think so,' Zam replied. 'If I asked you to kill Ackx,' he said to Hestia, 'could you do it?'

Hestia started to walk once more, making her way towards the steps. 'You said you were only going to ask me one more question.'

'That was only because you started to talk about light and God and started to get old and boring. Now I want to know if you could kill him.'

'Yes,' said Hestia. 'I could do that, but I never would.'

'Why not, you've killed before?'

'To cause that kind of death is the most horrifying thing you could ever ask me to do.'

'What's so different about killing Ackx?'

'He is my father,' Hestia said as she descended the last step and pushed the maintenance shaft door open with her muzzle. 'And if I kill him, then it is likely I will become just like him.'

21

The maintenance shaft was lit by inadequately spaced light bulbs covered in cobwebs and grime. It was like moving down a black burrow from one pocket of dimness to the next. The cramped space meant that Hestia had to shrink to the size of a normal tiger so that Zam didn't hit his head on the ceiling.

Zam watched Slink as he raced in and out of the dim lights ahead of them.

'Now I see me, now I don't,' Slink said, continuing on from the game of hide and seek he played outside.

'I'm glad Ackx is not my father,' Zam said to Hestia. 'How could you ever have helped him to do the things he does?'

Hestia remained silent as she slowly padded along and Zam decided it was best to do the same.

'There's a ghost door here,' Slink eventually yelled when he reached the end of the maintenance shaft. 'I don't like the feel of what's on the other side. We should turn around and go find some swings. I haven't been on a swing in ages.'

Zam reached the door a moment later, with a sickly feeling churning in the depths of his stomach. He chose to ignore it though and when Hestia silently opened the door they stepped inside, finding themselves once more within Mandrake Ackx's domain. They were deep in the dark shadows of the cavern, hidden from Ackx who was illuminated by the glare of a fiercely burning fire in the centre of the vast space.

Ezzy stood at his side holding his hand.

Zam stared intently at Ackx's crooked silhouette as he talked to Ezzy. 'I want you to kill Ackx,' Zam whispered to Hestia. That was his plan, since he first knew she could kill Ackx. He knew it was a bad plan, but it was better than his first idea which relied on Ackx transforming into Time and not being there when Zam eventually found Ezzy and Grandfather.

'I have brought you this far, that is as much as I can do,' Hestia replied in a hushed voice.

Zam detected a hint of regret in Hestia's voice as she spoke and wondered if she could be convinced otherwise. 'Looks like I'm going to die then,' he said, hoping she would feel sorry for him and kill Ackx anyway. Of course she didn't and instead, Hestia bent down for Zam to slide off her back. Zam reluctantly got off Hestia and leant into her side as he waited for his legs to get used to carrying his weight. He felt stiff from the ride and he could feel that his legs were not going to support him for long. He desperately missed Q, not just for the physical support, he wanted his friend back. Despite knowing Q for only a short while it felt like he had been a lifelong companion. It felt like he knew more about Q than he did about Grandfather or Ezzy put together.

Focusing his attention back towards the wyte, he watched as Ackx looked down at Ezzy and she in turn stared up at him in reverence. It made Zam sick to the stomach to see her this way. Eventually, dragging his eyes from them, he scanned the area looking for Grandfather.

'What have you got planned?' Hestia asked.

Zam crouched down and began to crawl nearer to Ackx. 'I want to hear what they are saying.'

'Then what?' Hestia asked, crawling beside him.

'I'm still working on then what.'

Zam couldn't see Slink in the shadows but when he spoke he realised Slink was crawling beside him too.

'This is great fun. I love playing hide and seek,' Slink whispered.

Zam had a thought. 'Could you look around the cavern for Grandfather?' he asked Slink.

'Yeah, that would be fun too,' Slink said, almost too loud. 'Who is Grandfather by the way?'

Zam sighed, 'Just look for an old man with a long beard. And do it quietly, we don't want to let Ackx know we are here.'

'Okay. I can do that,' Slink said and when he didn't say anything else, Zam assumed he must have left.

'This place seems different to the last time I was here,' Zam said to Hestia as he crawled towards Ackx once more.

'It changes all the time depending upon father's mood and who he is with.'

The ground felt slippery in places and Zam remembered the gloopy substance dripping from the ceiling when he was last inside the cavern. That part hadn't changed. He sniffed his hand and it smelled of boiled cabbage. He hoped the rest of his body didn't smell the same. 'If I can get Ezzy and Grandfather away from Ackx,' he said to Hestia, 'how do we get out of the underworld and back into our own world?'

'The same way you came in.'

'We entered by a door from Victoria Tunnel. The door isn't there anymore.'

'That door and others are always there. You just have to look in the right place.'

Zam was about to ask where the right place was when they moved to within earshot of Ackx and he dared not speak. While he had previously thought Ezzy was staring at Ackx with reverence, close up he now saw things differently. Her eyes were distant and he could see that she had been crying. Ezzy never cried, at least, he had never seen her cry until she came into the underworld. It made Zam all the more determined to make Ackx pay.

'Learn from his mistake, sweet child. Never lie to me,' Ackx said. 'Understand to do so, the consequences will be severe.' He spoke as if he was speaking to an infant.

'Let him go, please let him go and I promise I'll do anything you want me to.'

Ackx touched Ezzy's cheek with his delicately boned hand and Zam was surprised to see a kind expression on his bestial face. 'There is no need for me to do that child. You will always do what I want anyway.'

Ezzy's eyes widened and she raised her foot while Ackx continued to stare at her, 'You really think so?' she said as she stamped on the top of Ackx's bare foot. 'See if a broken metatarsal changes your mind.'

Ackx's expression changed to a look of complete agony as he shrieked and bent down, grabbing hold of his foot. Then his whole body began to disfigure as he raised himself up to his full height while continuing to hold onto his foot.

Without waiting to see what Ackx did next, Ezzy ran from him and disappeared into the shadows to the left of Zam.

'Follow Ezzy and get her out of here,' Zam ordered Hestia, before standing up and lurching towards Ackx.

Hearing Zam approach, Ackx turned around to face him but he was too late to stop Zam's charge. Barging into Ackx, Zam knocked the wyte to the floor, landing on top of him, attempting to pin him to the ground. Ackx quickly recovered and with disjointed, strobe-like movements he easily pushed Zam off, before crouching on top of him with a crab-like body shape.

'You have heart boy. I like that,' Ackx grinned manically.

It took all of Zam's resolve not to flinch away from Ackx's gaze and even more to speak. 'Where is my grandfather?'

'He is close,' Ackx smiled, turning towards the fire. 'He is very close.'

Zam followed Ackx's gaze, instinctively not wanting to see what the wyte was staring at, but knowing he must anyway. Grandfather was trapped inside the fire, silently screaming and writhing in continuous agony. He did not burn like the wood that fed the flames; he simply melted over and over again without ever losing his basic form and features.

'No!' Zam yelled, crawling from underneath Ackx and heading towards the fire. 'What have you done to him? Get him out of there.'

Ackx sat on the floor and studied his foot. 'Does this look broken to you?'

'Please, I'm begging you. Help him.'

'Do you know where my daughter went?'

'Yes, Hestia is with me, now please get Grandfather out of there.'

'Not Hestia, I meant my new daughter, Esmeralda.'

Zam noticed the body on the floor for the first time. It looked human in form, but aged as if it was 300 years old or more.

'Don't worry about him,' Ackx said. 'He's just an old friend of mine.'

The Relater lay discarded next to the body.

'He lied to me, your grandfather. The Relater does not work.'

Zam searched around the cavern, desperate to find something that could help Grandfather. There was nothing but darkness all around. 'If you kill Grandfather, the Relater will never work.'

A sharp snapping sound echoed around the cavern as Ackx suddenly wrenched his foot back into its normal shape. 'Who said anything about killing him? I simply teach a lesson.'

'He's learned his lesson. Me too. Now please put the fire out.'

'Where is my daughter?'

'I am here,' Hestia said as she walked into the fire light in the form of the young girl.

Ackx looked up from his foot. 'It wasn't you I was looking for.'

'I, too, have learned a lesson, Father.'

Ackx jumped up from the floor with the agility of a ballet dancer and began to circle Hestia without speaking.

Pulling his sleeve over his hand, Zam started to wrench logs from the fire, throwing them into the shadows, lighting up the cavern as he did.

'What have you learned?' Ackx eventually asked Hestia.

Hestia remained unmoving as Ackx continued to circle her. 'That choices are sometimes not really choices.'

'That's a valuable lesson to learn. Do you know where the green-eyed girl hides?'

'She hides in the shadows.'

'Would you choose to bring her to me?'

'No. I would not do that.'

Zam continued to remove more of the burning logs from the fire and it eventually collapsed in on itself, becoming a circle of glowing embers. His efforts made no difference to Grandfather, who continued to burn inside flames that had nothing to do with fire. Zam turned back towards Ackx and Hestia. 'Kill him, Hestia. It's the only way to help Grandfather.'

Hestia turned towards Zam. 'I will not kill my own father. No matter how much I want to, I can never do that.'

'Then stop Grandfather from burning,' Zam said, looking around for a weapon to use against Ackx. He glanced at the Relater and took a deep breath.

Hestia looked incredibly fragile as she turned away from Zam and gazed up at her father. 'The old man does not have to suffer anymore,' she said, grabbing hold of Ackx's hand.

Ackx squeezed her hand tightly. 'I do not want to be the same as my father.'

'I know.'

'Do you think I am like him?'

'I think we are all psychotic, the children of the underworld.'

'Do I frighten you, child?'

'You have always frightened me.'

A black tear trailed down Ackx's cheek. 'What is it about me that frightens you?'

Hestia bowed her head. 'Knowing that I am the same as you, Father.'

The sound of burning echoed around the space and the smell of smouldering logs filled Zam's nostrils as a small boy, no more than five years old, stepped out of the shadows holding aloft one of the logs like a torch. He walked towards Zam, who thought he recognised the boy, but couldn't quite place him.

Ackx stared at the boy for a moment then turned back towards Hestia. 'I know what it is like to lose a father.'

The boy reached Zam and gestured for him to bend down. Zam leant into him and the boy whispered into Zam's ear. 'I didn't find your grandfather, but I found Yelena.'

'Slink?' Zam said.

'She said you must not get overwhelmed. It's important that you only listen to one voice.'

Zam straightened up, trying to work out what Slink meant.

'I have to go now. Yelena is waiting for me. She said she knows a place where rollercoasters rise and fall between tropical thunder clouds.'

'Go to her, Slink. And thank you for all the help you've given me.'

'I remember everything now. Nothing is as straightforward as it first seems.'

Zam listened to Slink talk, but he stared at Ackx all the while and when Slink walked towards Eli and waved goodbye to him before disappearing into the shadows forever, Zam never saw him leave.

Instead, he picked up the Relater and walked as best as he could towards Ackx.

22

If it hadn't been for the puddle of gloop on the floor, Zam wouldn't have slipped and he would have put the Relater on Ackx's head, hoping it would age him like it had Slink. Once he was dead, Zam then hoped the fire engulfing Grandfather would die too.

As it happened, as soon as his foot touched the gloop he slipped and lost his balance, falling backwards. Thinking only of helping Grandfather, he desperately tried not to drop the Relater, gripping it tightly until he hit the ground. The force of the fall pushed his head towards the Relater he clung onto, yet even then he should have been safe. The dark life form his grandfather had created seemed to have a mind of its own though, as if it desperately wanted to attach itself to someone and like a snake hunting rats, it slithered from his hands, gaped wide open and engulfed Zam's head.

Everything instantly turned black and for just a moment, no more than a second, it was perfectly silent.

Then the voices started to sound one after another, after another, after another. All kinds of voices in all kinds of languages. Men, women, children and the supernatural. Every voice that had ever spoken and every voice destined to speak sounded out loud in Zam's head, until he was filled with shouting, whispering, crying.

Dying.

Zam felt himself changing, as if all of the experiences of the people behind the voices pounding inside his head were simultaneously happening to him right there and then. He remembered what Slink had said about the Relater overwhelming him, how it aged him and now he knew exactly how that was possible. He tried to tell his hands to move up to his head and wrench it off, but he couldn't feel them. All he could feel were the voices inside his head.

Yelena came to mind. *"It's important you only listen to one voice when there are lots of voices inside your head."* Zam heard her amongst the throng before she was quickly drowned out by another voice and another. He tried to concentrate on what she said but his mind couldn't do anything but listen to people generating time eternal. How could he listen to only one voice when there were so many of them inside his head? People talked excitedly, sorrowfully and joyously. Mostly, they talked mundanely. So mundanely that Zam began to feel claustrophobic.

Think of something else, he told himself in a voice he almost didn't recognise. *Think of Grandfather burning instead.*

Be strong.

Be strong for Grandfather.

How could he be strong when there was so much out of his control?

Listen to only one voice.

He tried and tried with all his will to listen to just one voice. He tried to listen to his own voice and no other. It was impossible. He couldn't concentrate. He couldn't hear his own voice because of all the other voices echoing inside his head. He could feel himself slipping into a place he didn't want to go. Slipping into oblivion where there was nothing but everything screaming for attention within his head.

All the voices the same, the same, the same.

Xyz, xyz, xyz...

One voice was different to the others – not so different in sound – it was more what the voice said. There, right on the edge of Zam's perception, this voice talked about Titan.

Titan, the largest moon of Saturn.

At first he thought it was Professor Brian Cox talking on TV, but it wasn't, it was the voice of an astronaut and the more Zam listened to what the astronaut said, the less he heard any other voice. Until, eventually, one fraction of a second at a time, Zam became the astronaut whose voice overwhelmed all other voices.

Ackx turned around just as Zam fell to the ground, and stared at the Relater as it swallowed Zam's head whole.

Even if he wanted to help the boy, he could not. He had never been afraid of anything in his life other than his father, yet the Relater frightened him more than his father ever could. The thought of growing old constantly gnawed at Ackx since first the Relater dropped off Benjamin and he saw how it had aged him. And now the boy's destiny was complete, just as he had foreseen after listening to the seductive voice of Time. Soon, the child would be a man, then an old man and finally, just before the boy turned into a withered corpse, Time's secret would be revealed to Ackx.

All in the time it took for you to consider your own sanity.

When Zam disappeared right in front of him, Ackx's eyes blinked rapidly and he turned to Hestia who had been watching with the same curious fascination. 'Time is the eternal deceiver,' he said, no longer smiling.

23

'Happy Christmas, Derrick,' a voice crackled through the speaker. The astronaut gazed down at the monitor on the panel festooned with dials and knobs, watching the flickering video image of the woman who had just spoken through static feedback. He ran a system check and looked up as an unfamiliar sound beat against the landing craft's fuselage. It mixed melodic with the irregular creak of the vessel as it rapidly cooled in the freezing atmosphere.

Zam couldn't begin to explain how it happened, but he was now connected to the astronaut called Derrick, like a cosmic voyeur in the neuron pathways of the man's brain. Everything Derrick experienced, so too did Zam; seeing through the astronaut's eyes and feeling with his fingertips while still holding onto his own self-awareness. He was certain the astronaut was not conscious of Zam inside his spirit. It would have surely sent him into a wild frenzy if he had been aware. Instead, the astronaut Zam carried out his duties like nothing had changed. Zam flicked a switch on the panel and watched as the heat shields slowly opened. Gazing out of the cockpit into the moonscape, he saw that Titan was hazy and yellow.

And it was raining methane drops.

'Is everything all right?' the crackle voice asked.

Watching rain falling in gravity so low that Zam could almost fly in it himself, he tingled all over inside the man's body. Methane raindrops on Titan were the size of small pebbles and fell in slow motion, like snowflakes falling in still winter air. Each drop wavered as it refracted sunlight into a spiralling prism and when the drops eventually landed, they gently burst into a new, near static life. Staring at infinite drops of liquid sunlight falling all around, Zam barely heard his new astronaut voice say, 'Everything is more than all right.'

As soon as the words left his mouth Zam was no longer the astronaut called Derrick. He was no longer on Titan. He was in a universe of white light.

'God? Is that you?' a musical voice asked. The voice was singular, but sounded like every other voice Zam had ever heard before. Not only did the voice sound, he could feel and taste it too and he saw it like a sunrise in a dark winter sky. And he could walk, his legs were just like everyone else's. Though he wasn't sure what it was he walked upon. Everything was white; there was no shape or shadows, nothing but the white light and Zam.

'I'm not God, if it's me you're asking,' Zam hesitantly replied.

'I thought... Oh, it doesn't matter. He has not spoken to me in an age.'

'I don't think God has spoken to anyone in an age. If He ever did speak to anyone to begin with.' Zam suddenly felt a force pressing on his shoulders after he spoke. A force now pressing against every part of his body, like he was about to be pressed into himself.

The pressure soon stopped and relieved, Zam breathed in deeply.

'Now I see you,' the musical voice said. 'Yes, you are Napoleon Xylophone.'

'Why did you think I was God?'

'I hear no other voice but His. And now I hear only yours.'

'Who are you?'

'He called me Zmanim.'

'Who is He, God?'

'That's a weird question to ask in these circumstances.'

Zam laughed, but he wasn't sure why. 'What did you and God talk about?'

'The places free will takes people mostly, and other things I no longer care to remember.'

'I think God should have called you Slink, not Zee.'

'He did not call me Zee.'

'That's a weird response to give in these circumstances.'

There was a pause before the voice spoke again. 'You are starting to sound like Him. Are you sure you are not really God?'

Zam gazed around, still seeing nothing but white light. 'Since I first got up this morning, I'm not sure about anything anymore.' He suddenly remembered Grandfather and Ackx and more. 'Where am I, Zee? I need to get back...' Then he thought about Yelena and Slink. 'Am I dead?'

'No. It is not your time yet.'

Time.

The Relater.

Zam quickly raised his hands to his head. The Relater wasn't there. 'I think I know you too, Zee. You are Time, right?'

'Why do you need to get back?'

'You don't know?'

Time paused for a moment while it searched. 'Oh, I see.'

'Don't you see everything?'

'Almost everything, if I care to look.'

'Mandrake Ackx said you are restless. You want to die.'

Time sighed. 'I grow weary, it is true.'

'Weary of what?'

'You heard the same things I hear. Day after day after day. You know how monotonous it all sounds.'

'I thought you said you only hear God talking. And now me, of course.'

'The other voices I hear, but I don't listen to them anymore.'

'Are you sure you aren't God?'

'I wish you hadn't asked that question.'

'Why not?'

'Because I don't know how to answer it.'

'Don't you make the rules? Can't you make things different?'

'I am part of the rules, I do not make them. I am no more than a thought, every thought. Without perception, awareness, I would not exist.'

'Mandrake Ackx wants to make things different. He wants to become you. Is that possible?'

'Everything that can be imagined is possible.'

Zam looked around, wanting to see who he was talking to. There was still nothing but white light. 'Do you want him to become you?' He eventually asked.

'I want nothing more than to speak to God.'

'Maybe He hears you, but doesn't listen anymore,' Zam said. 'Maybe God is dead.' The light started to change. It moved and shadows appeared. Colours seeped out of the shadows and formed a pathway of leaves. Purple leaves, orange, green and brown leaves. Other colours Zam could not name. Colours he had never seen before. And they crunched underfoot, making noises that leaves couldn't possibly make. Like they were speaking the sound they made as Zam's footsteps passed over them.

'He is not dead.'

The path twisted upside down and as Zam continued to follow it, following Time's voice, he did not fall from the path. 'How do you know?'

'I still feel Him.'

'What does He feel like?' It felt like Zam was a thought. Like he had no body, but total awareness of everything, and he could create anything his imagination could envisage. Like rainfall on Titan, which now fell all around him. And he too could become a methane raindrop. But that wasn't what he wanted. He wanted to walk on a path of leaves that spoke sound, while rainfall fell in slow motion all around him as he spiralled upside down and sideways and upright. Walking all the while like a normal person walked.

'He feels different. Like something substantial is about to happen.'

Zam wanted to ask more questions, but the path started to flicker, the rain too, like he was blinking himself awake. And all colour disappeared, all shadow vanished until only white remained and Zam couldn't tell if he was upside down or upright.

'It's the Relater,' Time said. 'It needs to rest. Soon you will have to return.'

Zam began to panic. He wanted to go back and help Grandfather, but he didn't know how to stop Ackx. 'Can you kill Mandrake Ackx for me?' he cried out.

Time laughed and it was the most joyous thing Zam had ever heard in his life. So joyous, Zam almost stayed lost in Time.

'You could never kill a wyte, child. Instead of thinking of death, you need to think in terms of aging. The old cannot help but become less ambitious and more accepting as each minute ticks on by.'

'You're talking about the Relater, right? How do I get Ackx to wear it?'

'That is easy. Just tell him you spoke to Time and Time spoke back to you. And remember, half truths and lies are infinitely more believable than truth alone.'

'What do you mean? I don't understand what you mean.' The flickering slowed down as white turned to black and when Zam stopped hearing Time speak, he disappeared once more and for the briefest of moments was lost to all and everything.

24

'Wonderful, wonderful child,' Ackx said when Zam reappeared almost as instantly as he had disappeared.

The Relater slipped off Zam's head like mellifluous honey and slid onto the floor, deflated and seemingly sated.

'Did you speak to Time?' Ackx continued, with his skeletal fingers hungrily moving across Zam's body as he helped him into a sitting position.

Zam blinked himself into awareness and immediately searched for Grandfather. He was dismayed to see he continued to burn inside Ackx's underworld flames. 'Put out the flames, right now wyte, or you will learn nothing from me.'

Ackx froze for a microsecond and ordinarily Zam would not have noticed such a minute detail but, fresh from his conversation with Time, he took in everything and understood absolutely the full meaning of Ackx's involuntary gesture.

'Of course,' Ackx said and with a flick of his wrist in Eli's direction he murmured *'Arrêter,'* and the flames were no more. 'Did Time speak to you?' he continued excitedly.

Zam watched as Hestia walked over to Grandfather and began to comfort him. 'Is he okay?'

Hestia sniffed Eli's skin before answering. 'It will take time, but he will heal.'

Time, time, time. Everything revolved around time. Time was his friend now, his true friend. 'You were right,' he said to Ackx. 'Time is restless.'

Ackx's eyes narrowed as one of his hands remained on Zam's shoulder. 'Continue, child.'

Zam attempted to stand up, but he felt incredibly stiff and remained seated. 'Time is lonely.'

Ackx removed his hand from Zam's shoulder and began to pace around him, biting his nails with his pointed teeth. 'Time can't be lonely. Time is close to everyone. I mean everyone who has ever lived and everyone who is destined to live.'

Zam timed his response perfectly. 'God has stopped talking to Time.'

Hestia raised her head from Eli and looked towards Zam.

Ackx stopped pacing. 'Did Time actually say that to you?'

'Time spoke in the most beautiful voice I have ever heard. I could see Time's voice. Smell and touch it. How is that possible?'

Ackx snapped one of his nails off with his teeth and spat it to the ground. 'How did you control the Relater? You look as though you haven't aged a single minute.'

'Grandfather told you the Relater has always been able to communicate with Time.'

Ackx stopped pacing and bent his neck back, looking up to the cavern ceiling momentarily before eventually closing his eyes. 'Yes, but how did you control it? How did you stop it aging you?'

Half truths and lies, Zam thought. 'When you listen to Time, what does it sound like?'

Ackx opened his eyes and looked towards Hestia. 'Exactly as you said. It is more than something you hear. Time's voice is everything you can physically experience too. It is a favourite smell, a first taste from childhood, a vision shared with one you love. Time touches you as if it had fingers that possess infinite knowledge of how to caress with utmost beauty and you in turn can touch Time. You can feel its breath as if it was your own sleeping child's.'

Zam almost lost himself in Ackx's words. Staring at Grandfather focussed his mind. 'But you only hear one single voice?'

'Of course,' Ackx snapped, glaring down at Zam like he was about to strike him for being so obvious.

'Time is more than a single voice. Time is every voice ever spoken. You have to listen to all of Time's voices before it will listen to you.'

Ackx's head started to involuntarily jerk from side to

side. 'The boy…' He didn't finish what he was about to say; instead, he walked over to Hestia. 'Can I trust myself?' he asked his daughter.

'Of course you can't, Father. But you have no choice. This is your destiny.'

Ackx clenched and unclenched his fist. Then he bent down and started to retch black vomit. It burst from his mouth, landing near Hestia.

Zam stared at the Relater. No longer flat and lifeless, it had grown back to its normal shape and size. Taking a break didn't appear to be something it needed to dwell upon, he thought.

When Ackx finished retching he stood up tall and straight and far too stiff. 'Something is wrong,' he said. 'It cannot be this easy. It is never this easy.'

He was right, Zam thought, knowing it wouldn't be so easy to convince Ackx to put the Relater on his head. He had been thinking that way while Ackx retched and an idea came to mind to make it easier for Ackx to accept. Picking the Relater up, Zam started to crawl towards one of the burning logs.

Ackx watched him for a moment before speaking. 'What are you doing?'

'Nothing,' Zam replied as he continued to make his way towards the log.

Ackx got down on all fours and loped sideways towards Zam, like a crab chasing the tide.

Twisting around to make sure Ackx could reach it in

time, Zam threw the Relater towards the log. He threw it too well; it landed right next to the burning log and began to screech in a high-pitched wail that almost had Zam weeping in pity.

'What are you doing?' Ackx yelled, scurrying past Zam and dropping his walking cane as he pulled the Relater from the flames. Standing upright, he held it to his chest, hugging it like a baby, while at the same time patting out the flames that had so quickly threatened to burn it out of existence.

'It's dying anyway,' Zam said.

Half truth and lies.

Ackx moved across to Zam and kicked him in the side of his stomach. 'What do you mean? And don't lie to me or the consequences will be...'

'Severe. I know,' Zam gasped. 'I can see where Time is coming from when it speaks of sameness.'

Eli sat up in Hestia's arms. 'What he is trying to tell you, Mandrake, is that the Relater can only be used once.'

'Nonsense,' Ackx said. 'It has been used three times already and yet lives.'

Zam was overjoyed to see Grandfather speaking and, more so, that he understood immediately what Zam was trying to do. Seeing how weak he looked made his heart sink.

'It has only spoke to Time once; the other times it just listened. Being exposed to Time like Zam managed to do has taken too much out of the Relater.'

Ackx's face began to twitch. 'Why would you want to destroy the Relater if it was dying already?'

Eli closed his eyes and buried his head in Hestia's chest.

'It is you who is dying, old friend, not the Relater. Do not worry. Time will be kind to you when you depart this world,' Ackx smiled. 'I will be kind to you, old friend.' He looked down at the Relater, ready to place it on his head.

'No, wait!' Zam yelled, suddenly fearful he had been too reckless and done the wrong thing. 'What are you going to do when you become Time?'

Ackx held the Relater in his outstretched arms, staring at it, insanely pleased with himself. 'I'm going to make everyone the same as me, of course,' he said, placing the Relater on his head. It enveloped him in an instant and he instantly began to scream like only the psychotic scream.

25

Ackx did not disappear like Zam had when the Relater first engulfed him. Instead, he remained in the cavern with his head covered in a slick film of darkest sentience. With his features covered, Ackx's head was no more than an angular black skull and as his psychotic melodies echoed around the cavern, Zam instinctively shrank away from him.

Spinning around and around, Ackx frantically tried to wrench the Relater from his head. It would have been easier to rip his own skin from his face. Like Ackx, the Relater had become greedy since feeding on Time and it relentlessly ate into Ackx's mind as he stumbled across the cavern floor in jerking movements his body should never have been capable of making. When Ackx finally stopped screaming and began to talk in innumerable voices, Zam hoped he was finished. A moment later, Ackx found his own voice and Zam knew his optimism had been misplaced.

'Xylophone!' Ackx yelled as he loped across the floor on all fours, hunting for Zam. Despite having no eyes now that the Relater covered them, he seemed to have an in-built sense of Zam's location.

Scrambling away from him, Zam's hand brushed against the walking cane. He picked it up and it burned as he clasped the smooth-boned shaft in his hand. Ackx was upon him as soon as the burning sensation first tingled his fingers and Zam swung the walking cane almost without thinking. The hoof of the cane connected perfectly with the side of Ackx's head, sending him sprawling across the floor. Ackx immediately got up and sprang back towards Zam, who began to jab at Ackx with the cane, using it like a spear in an attempt to keep him away.

'You would strike me with my own father's bones?'

Before he could answer, Ackx lunged, landing on top of Zam and pinning him to the ground with his weight. Zam could do no more than stare up at Ackx, as he opened his mouth impossibly wide beneath the stretching skin of the Relater, until eventually his teeth tore through it. Then he snarled hideously and leant into Zam with his teeth almost touching Zam's face, like he was about to chew it off.

Ackx never got the opportunity to finish what he had started, thanks to Ezzy, who stood behind him with a burning log in her hands. She swung the log wildly, smashing it into the side of Ackx's chest. 'You are not my father,' she tearfully yelled, as she then thrust the burning log into Ackx's face. The Relater immediately burst into flames and while Ackx screamed in a new kind of pain, Zam forced the hoof of the walking cane deep into the wyte's gaping maw.

Standing upright, Ackx pulled the bloody cane from his mouth and threw it to the ground. Then he frantically started to pat his head in an attempt to put out the flames. Zam rolled away from him as the Relater burned like it was impregnated with car fuel and Ackx screamed in a multitude of different voices, as if Time itself came from his mouth.

Kneeling down beside Zam, Ezzy hugged him with her eyes closed as Ackx shrieked his way from one end of the cavern to the other until finally, he slumped to the ground, silent and immobile while the Relater continued to burn as though it would never go out.

'Is he dead?' Ezzy finally asked.

'I think so,' Zam whispered, not wanting to turn his eyes towards Ackx.

Hestia gently stroked Eli's forehead. 'Rest now,' she said and Eli closed his eyes like he had no other choice. She stood up and walked across to her father. 'Arrêter,' she breathed when she reached him. The flames consuming Ackx's head immediately ceased and Hestia gasped when she saw her father's face.

'Is he dead?' Zam asked, still holding onto Ezzy. 'Is it over?'

'No, he is not dead, but it is over.'

'He isn't dead?'

'He is old. Too old to care. That is what finished him, not the flames.'

Reluctantly, Zam disentangled himself from Ezzy and stood up unsteadily. Ezzy joined him and held onto him as they walked across to Grandfather. When they reached him, Zam saw he was unscathed by the flames that had consumed him earlier. He looked terribly fragile, though, like he too had been aged by the Relater.

'Is Grandfather going to be okay?'

Hestia crouched down and kissed her father's forehead and Zam saw that Ackx had not been as fortunate as Grandfather. His face was melted away by the flames; half of his skin was red raw, the other half black Relater.

'Only time will tell,' Hestia said as she began to weep for her father.

26

Zam looked out of the apartment window across Newcastle's cityscape. His Newcastle, not the Newcastle of Mandrake Ackx's underworld. The sky was grey; it looked like it would rain before he set off for school. Zam didn't mind; a grey skyline these days was more preferable to a red sky.

Mostly.

It had been over a month since Hestia had carried Zam and Grandfather back from the underworld and left them to come to terms with their individual experiences. Zam was glad he hadn't seen Hestia since. Despite her help, he didn't think he could ever forgive her for what she had done to Rat.

It was also over a month since he had last seen Ezzy, apart from at school. She said she needed time to think, but mostly she needed to look after her mum. Zam kept sending her stupid photographs he'd taken on his mobile phone of John Lewis' mannequins he'd moved around the store. He set them up in different poses, changing a head for a cabbage, having one eating a sandwich while watching TV or showing one picking its nose while wearing a lopsided lampshade as a hat, which was kind of difficult as none of the mannequins had a nose. He hoped that making them ridiculous would make Ezzy not so frightened of them, but she rarely answered his texts.

Looking after Grandfather kept him occupied. At first, Zam thought Grandfather was never going to recover – he seemed as distant as Ezzy – but eventually he started to talk again and lately he had been in his workshop where he allowed Zam to watch him tinker. He still wouldn't go anywhere near fire. Zam couldn't imagine what it must have felt like to be engulfed like Grandfather in underworld flames.

Grandfather sat reading in his new rocking chair designed and built by his new technical assistant – Jha Round. *"Anyone who can create something like this needs to be working with me,"* Grandfather had said two days previously, when Jha delivered it as a surprise birthday gift from Zam. The chair was curvaceous and constructed from walnut with fittings made from a reclaimed naval mine. The velvet seat cover had once been part of a Victorian gentleman's smoking jacket. The arms of the coat had been chewed away by mice in Hancock Museum's basement. Jha knew a cleaner who worked there and when he found the remains of the coat in a bin, he guessed Jha would find a use for it.

"Everything of interest has some history behind it," Jha had said in his Polish accent. *"I only use materials of interest in my designs."*

'I need the dongulator,' Grandfather suddenly said, looking up from the book he was reading, 'do you still have it?'

'The what?' Zam said, removing his earphones. He had been listening to Mok, a new indie group Jha was obsessed about. Jha was obsessed about all of his music, but Zam really liked Mok. He listened to them more than he listened to The Clash lately, which was a real surprise to him.

'The device I put in your pocket after Mandrake destroyed Q.'

'Oh that. I wondered what it was.'

'Do you still have it?'

'Yeah. I guess. It's in my bedroom. Somewhere.' Zam said, continuing to stare out the window at the sky.

'It's important you find it.'

'Why?'

'I won't be able to bring Q back without it.'

Zam spun around in the walking frame. 'What do you mean?'

Grandfather closed the book, 'Before Mandrake touched Q, I downloaded his memory into the dongulator using its wifi capability. Everything Q experienced since you first met him is stored on it. I intend to download Q into the memory banks of a new improved wheelchair I'm going to make for you with Jha.'

'A new Q?' Zam said, smiling for the first time in a long time.

'No, it's the same old Q, if you still have the dongulator. It's just the wheelchair that's going to be new.'

Zam steadied himself in the walking frame and moved towards his grandfather. 'Are there other creatures like Mandrake Ackx?' he said, when he reached him.

Eli sighed, 'All the creatures in your worst nightmares and more are out there somewhere.'

Zam stared at the floor. 'You can't bring Rat back from the dead, can you?' he eventually asked.

'No, I cannot do that.'

'Since we returned,' Zam said, looking up at his Grandfather, 'I've been seeing these things, like shadows that move. Always in the corner of my eye. But every time I turn around, there is nothing there. If I didn't know better, I'd say Slink was playing hide and seek with me.'

'You have been subjected to the underworld, Napoleon. I can't say for sure, but there is a good chance it has awakened the clairvoyant blood inside you. You may be experiencing the spirit world like a seer does.'

'There's clairvoyant blood inside me?'

'Indeed, that would come from your grandmother.'

'You never talk about Grandmother.'

'No.'

189

Zam detected a tone in Grandfather's voice that meant he wasn't going to say any more about her and decided not to press him further, not yet. 'I don't want any more to do with the underworld or spirits.'

'Sometimes we do not have a choice.'

'Now you're beginning to sound like Hestia. You must be black, like she says she is, whatever that means.'

A half smile crossed Eli's face, 'That cannot be true. If Hestia is black, then I must be white.'

Zam's hands tightened around the walking frame. 'These shadows I see, or don't see. It feels like they want something from me.'

'I do not think it is anything to be afraid of, Napoleon. They are drawn to your energy, like they are drawn to the energy of every other living person on the planet. The difference is that you can see them.'

'I'm not afraid.'

'You need some guidance, an awakening clairvoyant has much to learn and understand. Hestia...'

'I don't want anything to do with Hestia. Ever again. She killed Rat, remember?'

Eli sighed, 'In that case, you should prepare yourself for dark times ahead. The dead may not be physically connected to our world, but they have other ways of interacting and they will seek to use you, once they know you can see them.'

Zam closed his eyes for a moment. When he opened them, Grandfather continued to stare at him. He turned around without speaking, heading for his bedroom – in need of a friend.

Knowing he would find one, once he found the dongulator.

Author Note

Napoleon Xylophone sprung to life from two independent sources. The first source came during a lecture as part of an MA in creative writing I undertook at Teesside University. During the lecture I was asked to develop a writing workshop directed at a group or organisation where I had an interest or affiliation. The second and most important source came from my eleven year-old son, Michael and the ambassador club he attended with Whizz-Kidz, a UK based charity working with disabled children. Michael has a walking disability which means he has to spend most of his time in a wheelchair. We often talked about the lack of disabled superheroes in fiction novels or in movies and I saw this workshop as an opportunity to create a superhero for Michael and other disabled children. After discussing the idea with Whizz-Kidz they gave the go-ahead for me to run five workshops with their children based at Newcastle.

As well as creating a different kind of superhero, another aim of the project was to give disabled children a different kind of voice, one which allowed them to express how they fit into society without coming across as crusaders looking for sympathy. This new voice was spoken through a fifteen year old schoolboy called Napoleon Xylophone. Right at the start it was agreed that our superhero would not have special powers like Superman. Our hero needed to use his wits and gadgets like Batman to help get himself out of trouble. As he travelled through the pages of his story, Napoleon shows the difficulties disabled children encounter in everyday life. Issues such as people staring, bullying, difficulties getting into shops, onto public transport or simply crossing the road were all discussed by the children.

During the workshops we also looked at characterisation and plot, with the children putting forward suggestions for story development as well as character names. Mandrake Ackx was one of the names they suggested, along with supernatural creatures such as changelings and ghosts with bad memories.

After completing the workshop and coming up with some great ideas, it seemed a shame to leave *Napoleon* unpublished. No mainstream publisher was going to publish a book like *Napoleon Xylophone* and after failing to obtain support from the Arts Council, we decided to publish his story ourselves. That was when the second part of Napoleon's adventure started with fundraising activities that included a sponsored walk along an eighteen mile stretch of water by the banks of the river Tees. The journey took the participants from Bowes Museum at Barnard Castle to Broken Scar near Darlington town centre. Funds raised from the walk along with a contribution from a local firm meant we had enough money to self-publish Zam's story.

I hope you enjoyed his story and perhaps got a small insight into what life is like in a wheelchair.

Acknowledgements

Those involved in the creative writing workshops at Newcastle including: Rebecca Farren, Ellen Law, Adam Clarke, Brigit Hobson, Damian and Nathan Pearson, Jack Bell, Jake Oakes, Hilary Morgan, Emma Booth, Rachael Rich, Daniel Miller, Michael Simpson, Ruth Madeley and Sue Balf. Thanks also, for all the encouragement from the carers who attended the workshops as well as Sally Waters and Ashley Westpfel for driving through the final publication activities.

Many thanks to the following for completing the sponsored walk and helping to raise enough funds to enable *Napoleon Xylophone* to be published: Craig Noel, Mark Poole, Gary Greenwell, Graham Welford, Rachel Lewin, Ross Killip, Shaun Briddick and Adrian Crowe – the backup driver and provisions man!

For all the encouragement and suggestion from my friends at FS, with special thanks to Polly Pisces, Moyramouse and Stu.

Thanks to the following lecturers who guided and helped me through both the workshop process and for getting me to think differently about writing: Bob Beagrie, Andy Willoughby, Carol Clewlow, Chris

Thurgar-Dawson and especially Nasser Hussain who got what Napoleon was all about from the very first page and brought a little steampunk to the feel of the novel.

A big thank you also to Karen, Amy, Caitlin, Michael, Roxanne, Em, Zed, Debs – my very own Twitter marketers. And a special thanks to David who helped shape *Xylophone* as much as anyone else. Oh, and Rufus Hobster, how could I forget you?

If I have missed anyone I am truly sorry. Give me a shout and I'll buy you a coffee or a tea or just maybe – an underworld ice-cream.